TOMATOES,
POTATOES,
CORN,
AND BEANS

TOMATOES, POTATOES, CORN, AND BEANS

HOW THE FOODS OF THE AMERICAS CHANGED EATING AROUND THE WORLD

by Sylvia A. Johnson

illustrated with archival prints and photographs

Atheneum Books for Young Readers

For my family, who likes nothing better than cooking
and eating good food from around the world.

Atheneum Books for Young Readers
An imprint of Simon & Schuster Children's Publishing Division
1230 Avenue of the Americas
New York, New York 10020

An E. M. Petersen Book

Book design by Edward Miller.
The text of this book is set in Bembo 12/17.
Printed in the United States of America.
First Edition
10 9 8 7 6 5 4 3 2 1

Library of Congress Cataloging-in-Publication Data
Johnson, Sylvia A.
  Tomatoes, potatoes, corn, and beans : how the foods of the Americas
  changed eating around the world / by Sylvia A. Johnson — 1st ed.
  p. cm.
  Includes bibliographical references and index.
  Summary : Describes many foods native to the Americas,
   including corn, peppers, peanuts, and chocolate, that were taken to
   Europe and used in new ways around the world.
  ISBN 0-689-80141-6
   1. Cookery (Vegetables)—History—Juvenile literature.
   2. Vegetables—North America—History—Juvenile literature.
   3. Vegetables—South America—History—Juvenile literature.
   4. Vegetables—West Indies—History—Juvenile literature.
  [1. Cookery—Vegetables. 2. Vegetables.] I. Title.
  TX801.J64 1997   641.6'5'09—dc20   96-7207
  CIP   AC

Title page: Christopher Columbus leaves on his second voyage to the Americas. This drawing from 1621 pictures Ferdinand and Isabella watching (upper right) as the ships set sail for the New World.

CONTENTS

The title page from the 1633 edition of John Gerard's herbal. First published in 1597, this book contains some of the earliest European descriptions of food plants from the Americas. Gerard's work was influential, but it was not very accurate.

INTRODUCTION

What would Italian cooking be without the tomato? Can you imagine Indian curries without the peppers that give them their hot, spicy taste? What would German or Russian cooks do if they didn't have potatoes? And how would French chefs manage without chocolate to make mousses, éclairs, and other tempting desserts?

It's hard to imagine, isn't it? Yet for a very long time, cooks in Italy, India, and many other parts of the world didn't have any of these foods in their kitchens. Italians topped their pasta with sauces made of cream, cheese, or vegetables. "Hot" foods prepared in India and other Asian countries owed their fire to black pepper or to spices such as cumin, coriander, and ginger. And in many countries, sweets were made of milk, honey, and almond paste, ingredients that did not tickle the taste buds like dark, rich chocolate.

Chocolate came to Europe from the Americas in the 1500s. This illustration from a book published in 1688 shows an idealized Native American and, in the panel below him, the cacao plant, the source of chocolate.

Why didn't cooks in Europe or Asia have tomatoes, potatoes, peppers, chocolate, and other foods that seem so essential to cooking today? The reason is simple: The plants from which these foods come are not native to Europe, Asia, or any other part of the Eastern Hemisphere.

Many food plants *did* originate in this part of the world. Grains such as wheat, oats, barley, and rice were domesticated in Asia and became staples in the diets of millions. Vegetables such as carrots, peas, cabbage, eggplant; fruits such as apples, grapes, pears, peaches: all these foods were grown and eaten by people in the European countries, in India, China, and other parts of Asia, as well as in some areas of Africa.

But not tomatoes, potatoes, peppers, and chocolate. These are all foods of American origin. The plants that produce them are native only to the Western Hemisphere—to North, Central, and South America. Maize (corn), squash, peanuts, vanilla, and many kinds of beans also originated in the Americas. For centuries, people in Europe, Asia, and Africa had no contact with the continents of the Western Hemisphere. This distant part of the world, with its native peoples, animals, and plants, was completely unknown to them. But all that changed in 1492.

Everyone knows what happened in that famous year. Christopher Columbus and his followers, seeking a shorter route to the riches of the Indies, "discovered" the Americas. On the Caribbean island where they first disembarked, the travelers observed in wonder: "All the trees were as different from ours as day from night, and so the fruits, herbage, the rocks, and all things."[1]

Columbus insisted that these strange new lands were part of Asia. But later explorers quickly realized his mistake and proclaimed the discovery of a "New World." For the native inhabitants of the Americas, however, the invaders from Europe were the newcomers. Their world was not new but as ancient as the one from which the Europeans came.

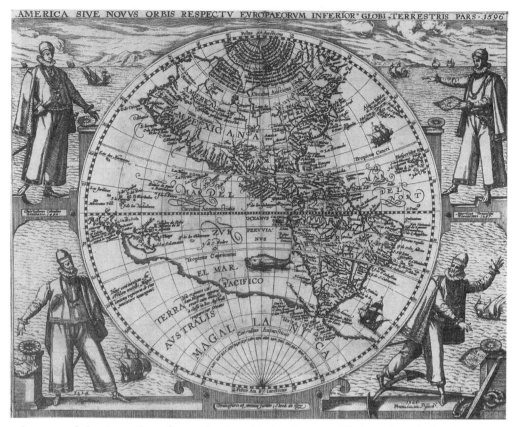

A map of the Americas from the late 1500s pictures Christopher Columbus (upper left) and Francisco Pizarro (lower right), two of the Europeans who "discovered" this new world. The other figures are Ferdinand Magellan (lower left) and Amerigo Vespucci (upper right)

Human beings had lived in the Americas for thousands of years before the arrival of Europeans. They made their homes in many different regions: in the cold Arctic, on sun-drenched plains, in tree-shadowed rain forests, on the slopes of high mountains. Some were hunters and gatherers who obtained their food from wild animals and plants. Others were farmers, tending cultivated fields that supplied food for single families, for tiny villages, or for great cities with thousands of inhabitants.

Native American farmers were well acquainted with the plants that grew in their world. In ancient times, they had domesticated wild plants to produce many varieties of maize, potatoes, beans, and squash. These basic foods became staples in large parts of the Americas. The fat red tomatoes and glossy peppers that seemed so exotic to early European explorers were familiar crops to many native farmers. And Native American cooks knew hundreds of ways to prepare and serve their grains, fruits, and vegetables.

After Columbus's expeditions, many other European adventurers made their way across the Atlantic to the Americas. For most of these people, the native foods of these new lands were only curiosities. Cortés, Pizarro, and the other Spanish conquistadores came to exploit the riches of the New World, and the treasure that they most desired was precious metal. They found gold in the temples of the Incas in Peru and silver in the mines of Mexico. But they paid little attention to the plants whose value would eventually prove to be far greater.

Despite this lack of interest, American plants slowly found their way to Europe, Asia, and Africa. Many were carried home by explorers as souvenirs or as scientific specimens. On return trips to the Americas, European settlers brought with them plants and animals from home. Wheat and barley were soon growing in American soil, and cattle grazing in the fields. Meanwhile, back in Europe, a few daring farmers were experimenting with the cultivation of maize and potatoes. An exchange had begun that would transform the lives of people in both worlds.

As we well know, contact between the Old World and the New had many tragic consequences. The European invaders killed and enslaved the native people of the Americas, destroyed their cities, and took their lands. Even more devastating were the epidemic diseases caused by bacteria that the newcomers unknowingly carried with them. In Aztec Mexico, for example, smallpox "spread over the people as great destruction. . . . Very many died of it. They could not walk; . . . they could not move; . . . nothing could be done

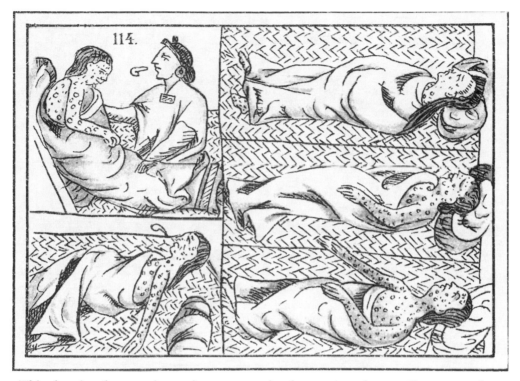

This drawing by a native artist portrays the devastation that smallpox caused among the Aztecs. The picture is part of the Florentine Codex, a historic document from the 1500s that presents a detailed account of Aztec life.

for them."[2] In some regions, as much as 90 percent of Native American populations died from smallpox, measles, and other European diseases to which native people had no immunity.

The meeting of two worlds that began in 1492 caused disruptions and upheavals still being felt today. But not all of the consequences were destructive. The exchange of foods between the Americas and the Old World improved the lives of millions. Because of it, people around the world ate better than they ever had before. Their diets were more nutritious and much more varied and interesting.

In this exchange, as in others, the Americas probably made the bigger contribution. Tomatoes, potatoes, maize, peppers, and chocolate transformed cooking and eating in large parts of Europe, Asia, and Africa. The American foods became essential to the nourishment and the eating pleasure of millions of people.

The story of how all this happened is one of the most fascinating chapters in world history.

Another drawing from the Florentine Codex shows Spaniards landing on the coast of Mexico in 1519, bringing with them horses, pigs, and other animals from Europe.

MAIZE
The American Grain

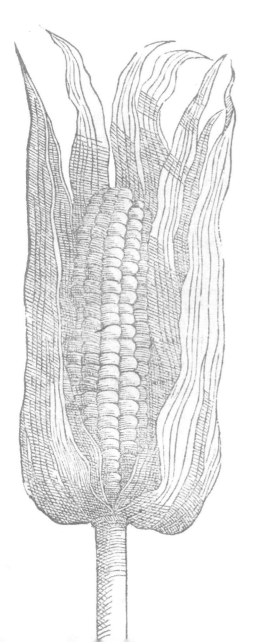

After a voyage that lasted three long months, Christopher Columbus and his shipmates reached the islands of the Caribbean on October 12, 1492. When they explored this unknown land (which they thought was part of Asia), the Europeans saw many strange new sights. They were particularly intrigued by one plant that they found growing in cultivated fields. It stood taller than a man and had ears thick as a human arm, covered with "grains in form and size like garden peas."[1] The plant was called *mahiz*, and the local Arawak Indians grew it for food. Columbus's son Ferdinand, who wrote an account of his father's adventures in the New World, reported that members of the expedition tried *mahiz*, or maize, and found it "most tasty, boiled, roasted, or ground into flour."[2]

A maize ear, from an Italian book about the Americas published in 1606

After Columbus's voyages, other Europeans set out to explore and exploit this strange new world and its resources. Almost everywhere they ventured in the Americas, they found maize.

In 1519, the Spaniard Hernán Cortés and his followers marched through the rugged lands of Mexico into Tenochtitlán, the capital of the Aztec empire. In the shallow lake surrounding the great city, they saw artificial islands, called *chinampas*, planted with maize, beans, and other food plants. The Spaniards were impressed by the variety of dishes that the Aztecs made from maize. There were breadlike tortillas thin as paper and all kinds of tamales made of soft maize dough wrapped around a filling—"wide tamales, pointed tamales,

Native Americans greet Columbus with gifts as he makes his first landing in the New World. This illustration pictures the scene through European eyes.

white tamales, . . . tamales with beans forming a seashell on top; . . . red fruit tamales, turkey egg tamales."[3]

Other Spanish conquerors led by Francisco Pizarro found maize as "tall as soldiers' pikes" growing in the land of the Incas in Peru. When they reached Cuzco, the Inca capital, in 1533, they saw maize plants made out of gold and silver in a garden next to the sacred Temple of the Sun. In the Inca markets, kernels of real maize were used as money. According to Spanish accounts, a woman shopping for food would put a small pile of maize on the ground next to the goods for sale and then add to the pile, kernel by kernel, until the seller was satisfied.

Not all Europeans who came to the Americas in the 1500s and 1600s were explorers and conquerors like Cortés and Pizarro. Some were settlers who had left the Old World in search of new homes. For these people, maize was more than just a curiosity. The American grain saved them from starvation and became a staff of life in a new and dangerous land.

The English colonists who arrived on the coast of North America in 1620 survived their first winter in the New World only because of the supply of maize they

Harvesting maize in Peru. From a series of drawings done by a native artist, Felipe Guaman Poma de Ayala, in the 1600s.

obtained from the Wampanoag Indians. Later the Wampanoag taught the settlers how to grow maize and prepare it for eating. William Bradford, the governor of Plymouth Colony, gave thanks to God rather than to his Native

Aztec farmers planting, cultivating, and harvesting maize. From the Florentine Codex.

American benefactors for the gift of maize: "And sure it was God's good providence that we found this corne for we know not how else we should have done."[4] (Today these words of Governor Bradford are inscribed on a monument erected at Corn Hill on Cape Cod, where the colonists found baskets of maize that had been hidden by the Indians.)

The Wampanoag, like most Native Americans, were skillful maize farmers. They had had long experience in cultivating this most important of food crops. Native farmers in North America planted maize seeds in hills of earth, along with dead fish to provide fertilizer. Beans were often planted in the same field or even in the same mound of dirt so that these two basic foods could grow together.

In Mexico, the Aztecs cultivated maize with methods that were centuries old. Friar Bernardino de Sahagún, a Spanish missionary who made a detailed study of Aztec life in the mid-1500s, describes the long, hard work of the maize farmer: "He hills [the maize plants], removes the undeveloped maize ears, discards the withered ears, breaks off the green maize stalks, . . . harvests the maize stalks, gathers the stubble; he removes the tassels, gathers the green maize ears, breaks off the ripened ears."[5]

Maize cultivation probably began in Mexico about eight thousand years ago. Like wheat and other grains, maize originated from a wild grass that was tamed by humans. Some scientists think that Native Americans developed modern maize from a kind of primitive maize plant. Others believe that a grass called teosinte is the direct ancestor of maize.

Still found in parts of Mexico and Central America, teosinte doesn't look much like the maize we know today. It is a small plant with several stalks, each bearing a single row of kernels enclosed in hard seed cases. But there is a close genetic relationship between the two plants, and scientists think that, by careful selection and breeding, early farmers could have developed a form of maize from the wild grass.

After its domestication in Mexico, maize spread quickly through the Americas. Around four thousand years ago, it was already being grown in Peru on the lower slopes of the Andes. Native Americans in what is now the southwestern United States learned maize cultivation from their Mexican neighbors. From there, the grain traveled throughout most of North America. By the time that Europeans arrived in the 1500s, native people from the Zuni and Hopi of the southwestern deserts to the Iroquois and Huron of the northeastern forests grew maize and depended upon it as a source of food.

Wherever maize was grown in the Americas, it was considered a sacred plant, a gift of the gods and a source of life. Many Native American religions included a god of maize. The ancient Maya, who were living in Mexico long before the Aztecs, revered the Young Maize God, often pictured in Maya art as a beautiful young man with maize tassels in his hair. According to a Maya story of creation, the gods had made early humans out of maize dough.

The people of the ancient Americas had many ways of honoring maize and the central role it played in their lives. For the Incas of South America, planting the first maize of the year was a religious ceremony performed by the Inca ruler, who used a foot plow made of gold to dig a hole for the seeds. Among the Hopi people of North America, every newborn child was given

The Native American town of Secota in Virginia, as seen by European artist John White in the late 1500s. On the right side of the picture are several fields of maize. The small structure marked F is a shelter used by watchers who guard the maize from hungry birds and animals.

a perfect ear of maize, called a Corn Mother, so that the sacred plant could bless the beginning of a new life.

The Hidatsa, who farmed along the banks of the Missouri River, sang as they cultivated their maize crop. As Buffalo Bird Woman, a Hidatsa who lived during the 1800s, explained, "We Indian people loved our gardens, just as a mother loves her children; and we thought that our growing corn liked to hear us sing, just as children like to hear their mother sing to them."[6]

Maize was a sacred plant to the people of the Americas, but it was also their daily bread, and much more. Native Americans cooked and ate maize in a great variety of ways, but there were some common themes.

Throughout North America, ears of maize picked while young were roasted or boiled (the original version of corn on the cob). The Choctaw and

Native Americans in Virginia eating a typical meal. The artist John White recorded that one of the dishes included "maize sodden, . . . of very good taste."

13

other North American tribes had Green Maize Festivals to celebrate the joyful time when the first tender ears were ready for eating. Sometimes kernels of young maize were cut from the cobs and combined with beans to make the dish we know today as succotash. Fresh maize was also dried or parched so that it could be stored and used later in stews and other cooked dishes.

Maize that was not picked green was left on the plant until it was firm and ripe. Then the crop was taken from the field and stored for future use. Friar Bernardino de Sahagún describes the way in which the Aztec farmer harvested his maize: "[He] shucks the ears, removes the leaves, binds the maize ears, . . . forms clusters of maize ears. . . . He fills the maize bins; . . . he spreads [the maize ears]. . . . He shells them, . . . cleans them, winnows them."[7]

Kernels of ripened maize could be cooked in hundreds of different ways. Most of these cooking methods started with boiling the hard kernels in water. The Maya and Aztecs of Mexico cooked maize kernels in water containing the mineral lime, which served to remove the tough outer hulls. Then they ground the softened maize with stone implements, producing a kind of dough. Today in many of the small villages of Mexico and Central America, maize is still prepared in this way, although women often take the cooked maize kernels to a commercial mill for grinding.

Maize dough provides the raw material for several basic dishes. Balls of the dough can be flattened and cooked on a hot griddle to make tortillas, a Spanish word that originally meant "little cakes." The Hopi people of the Southwest use a similar method to make a very thin, crisp maize cake called *piki*.

In ancient Mexico, tortillas were part of almost every meal and eaten with many other foods, just as they are in Mexico today. Friar Sahagún tells us that in the Aztec marketplace, hungry shoppers could buy tortillas "with shelled beans mashed, . . . with meat and grains of maize, . . . wrapped with chilli [peppers], . . . with turkey eggs."[8]

The dough produced by grinding softened maize could also be used to

An illustration from Girolamo Benzoni's book about the Americas shows the process of making maize tortillas. The woman on the right boils the maize in water containing lime, while the one on the lower left grinds the softened kernels to make a dough. The third woman cooks the tortillas on a griddle.

make tamales. Maya and Aztec cooks spread the dough on maize husks or other plant leaves and often added a filling—for example, beans and squash seeds. Then the husks were wrapped in little bundles, securely tied, and steamed or baked in the coals of a fire.

In North America, cooks removed the hulls from ripe maize by boiling the maize in water containing ash from burned wood. The resulting soft kernels, called *rockahomonie* in an Algonquian language, were cooked in stews along with meats and other ingredients. They could also be pounded or ground to make a kind of flour.

Ancient Native Americans also consumed cooked maize in the form of a liquid. In Mexico, the Maya and Aztecs mixed the softened and ground maize kernels with water to make a kind of thin porridge or gruel. With added ingredients such as ground peppers, beans, honey, and chocolate, this beverage was one of the basic foods of ordinary Maya and Aztec people. People in modern Mexico and Central America drink a similar maize beverage called *atole*.

The Incas had a maize drink called *chicha*, which was intoxicating. According to Spanish accounts, some forms of this beverage were "as strong or even stronger than wine."[9] Made from fermented maize, *chicha* was a kind of beer that was also very nourishing. The beverage was one of the most common ways of preparing maize among the Incas, whose diet was centered on another basic food of the Americas, potatoes. (In Peru, maize beer is still a common drink.)

One final way of preparing maize should seem very familiar to us today. Ancient Native Americans from Mexico to New England ate maize kernels popped over hot fires. The Wampanoag brought popped maize to the harvest feast that we call the first Thanksgiving. In Mexico, Aztec women wore garlands of popped maize on their heads like wreaths of flowers.

The Europeans who established settlements in the Americas during the 1600s and 1700s soon learned some of the methods of maize farming and cooking developed by Native Americans. They too came to depend upon maize as a food source, but at first many of them were not very impressed by this new grain.

The biggest problem was that maize could not be used to make the kind of bread products with which Europeans were familiar. The grain did not contain gluten, which is the protein in wheat that, combined with yeast, makes bread rise. In Mexico, the Spanish reluctantly learned to eat tortillas and tamales. Settlers in North America adapted Native American recipes to make fried hoecakes and pones out of ground maize mixed with eggs and water.[10] But these substitutes for the familiar loaf of wheat bread did not please many of the Europeans who were making new homes in a new world.

Europeans in Europe were even less impressed by this strange new grain. Maize arrived in Europe soon after Columbus's expeditions, probably brought by Spanish and Portuguese explorers. By the mid-1500s, it had reached the countries of western Asia, Africa, and even China. Most inhabitants of these regions didn't know what to make of the exotic American plant.

This early confusion about maize is reflected in the names given to it. At first, many Europeans connected maize with wheat, a grain they knew well, and they referred to it as Turkey or Turkish wheat. Why was the American grain called by this inaccurate name? No one knows for sure, but it may have been because maize was brought to some areas of Europe by merchants and traders from Turkey. Another possibility is that many Europeans associated almost anything new and exotic with the country of Turkey, which was ruled by the "infidel" Ottoman Turks. (A bird native to the Americas probably got its name for the same illogical reason.)

When maize was introduced in England, it was often referred to as Turkish

Turcicū frumentū. Tórckſch Corn

This drawing from an herbal by Leonhart Fuchs, published in 1543, is one of the first pictures of maize to appear in Europe. The labels refer to the American plant as "Turkish Grain."

corn rather than Turkish wheat. The English word *corn* originally meant "a small particle or grain" (this meaning has been retained in the word *peppercorn*). The term also came to be used for grain crops such as wheat, rye, and oats. Sometimes *corn* referred to whatever grain was grown in a region, for example, wheat. Among English-speakers in North America, however, corn gradually came to mean *only* maize. In the United States today, this usage continues. The original Native American word has almost been forgotten, even though it is still used in other parts of the world.

Whether it was called Turkish corn or Turkish wheat, maize was generally considered a poor excuse for a grain when it arrived in Europe during the 1500s. John Gerard, a well-known English gardener and amateur botanist, used some very harsh words when he described it in an herbal (an early book about plants) first published in 1597:

> Turky wheate doth nourish far less than either Wheate, Rie, Barly, or Otes. The bred which is made thereof is meanely white, without bran: it is hard and dry as Bisket is. . . . The barbarous Indians which know no better are constrained to make a virtue of necessitie, and think it a good food; whereas we may easily judge that it nourisheth but little, and is of hard and evil digestion, a more convenient food for swine than for man.[11]

Despite such negative reactions, it did not take long for people in at least some parts of the world to discover that maize could be a useful food plant. For one thing, it was very productive compared to other grains. An acre of land planted with maize produced about twice as much food as an acre of wheat. Maize also had a shorter growing time than most European grains, so its food was available sooner. And fewer hours of labor were needed to produce the American grain.

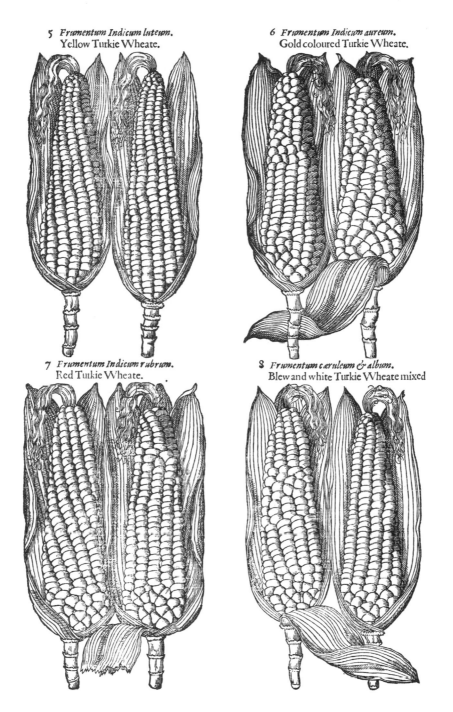

5 *Frumentum Indicum luteum.*
Yellow Turkie Wheate.

6 *Frumentum Indicum aureum.*
Gold coloured Turkie Wheate.

7 *Frumentum Indicum rubrum.*
Red Turkie Wheate.

8 *Frumentum cæruleum & album.*
Blew and white Turkie Wheate mixed

When John Gerard's famous herbal was republished in 1636, American maize was still known as "Turkie Wheate."

Another useful characteristic of maize was that it could be grown in many climates and under many different conditions. In the Americas, it was cultivated in high mountain valleys and in fields carved out of swamps. Some varieties thrived in desert heat, while others were adapted to cooler northern climates. When maize began to spread in Europe, farmers soon discovered that it could be grown in areas where conditions were unsuited to wheat and other grains.

Despite its many good features, maize did not become a common food crop in Europe. People in most areas continued to rely on wheat products for their basic diets. Maize came to provide food only for those people who did not have land for growing wheat and other grains and who could not afford to buy grain products. In the non-American world, maize found a place mainly as a food for poor regions and poor people.

By the early 1600s, peasant farmers in Spain and Portugal were probably growing maize. In the 1670s, the English philosopher John Locke saw fields of maize during his travels in southern France. He learned that the grain was called *ble d'Espagne* (Spanish wheat) and that it served "poor people for bred."[12]

Maize also became an important food crop in northern Italy, in the Po River Valley and the region near Venice. Here it was known as *granoturco* (Turkish grain) and was grown in areas too wet for millet and wheat. In southeastern European countries such as Romania and Hungary, poor people also discovered that maize was a cheap and productive source of food. For most of the rest of Europe, the American grain was considered good enough only to feed cattle and pigs.

Once some Europeans started growing maize for human consumption, they had to figure out how to cook it. Most of the cooking methods used by Native Americans did not travel to Europe. Europeans did not make tortillas and tamales or eat fresh maize in the form of succotash and "corn on the cob." Instead they cooked finely ground maize with water to make a kind of mush or porridge. This was a very ancient method of preparing grains that had been used in Europe for centuries.

In northern Italy, maize mush was called polenta, a name that came from an old Latin word for porridge. The German writer Goethe, who visited the area in the 1780s, noticed that peasant families ate polenta every day, "just as it is or sometimes with a sprinkling of grated cheese."[13] The thick, hot mush was usually poured out of the cooking pot onto a wooden board, where it was left to cool for a few minutes before being cut with a piece of thread or string. The slices of golden polenta would be firm on the outside but soft and warm inside.

As polenta became more and more popular, Italian cooks came up with many different ways of preparing it. It was eaten like pasta, topped with sauces made from mushrooms or tomatoes and peppers (also foods from the Americas). Milk and sugar or honey was added to hot polenta to make a breakfast porridge. Cold polenta was sliced and then fried in oil or baked in an oven.

In Romania, maize mush was called *mamaliga*; in the Transylvanian region of Hungary, *puliszka*. Cooks in these countries too found different ways to serve this basic dish. It was sometimes fried in butter or topped with sour cream and cheese made from sheep's milk. Many Romanian families served *mamaliga* just as Italians did polenta. They poured it from the cooking pot onto a board or right onto the scrubbed wooden table and cut it with a piece of string.

In Europe, maize became a common food only in limited areas. In Africa, however, millions of people came to depend on the American grain. Maize was first brought to Africa as a result of the international slave trade. This shameful traffic in human beings began in the 1400s, when Portuguese traders came to the west coast of Africa and took Africans to be sold as slaves in Europe and the Middle East. When European countries established settlements in the New World during the 1600s, the demand for slaves increased

Maize growing in a village in central Africa during the 1700s. A high wall of brush surrounds the village and its fields.

greatly. For almost three hundred years, slave ships crossed the Atlantic, transporting thousands of Africans to the plantations of the Americas.

On the return trip to Africa, early slave traders brought maize from the New World. At first, the grain was grown in West Africa to provide a cheap and convenient food for slaves being transported to the Americas. But gradually people in many areas of Africa began to cultivate maize for their own use. As in Europe, it filled a need for a food crop that was easy to grow and produced a high yield.

African cooks, like those in Europe, usually ground maize and cooked it with water to make a mush or porridge. Today millions of Africans still depend on maize mush for their basic food, eating it with spicy sauces and stews. In Ghana, it is called *kpekple*, while in parts of present-day Zaire, it is known as *bidia*. The people of Zimbabwe eat *sadza*, while East Africans have *posho* or *ugali*. In South Africa, Zulu-speaking people enjoy *putu*. Other South Africans eat mealie-meal mush (*mealie* is a local name for maize derived from a Portuguese word for another grain, millet).

Just as the slave trade originally brought maize to Africa, it also contributed some maize dishes to the cooking of the Americas. Black slaves transported to the islands of the Caribbean brought with them African ways of preparing maize, along with some traditional ingredients. One African dish called *coo-coo* combined maize mush with okra, a green vegetable native to parts of Africa. Slaves brought okra with them to the Caribbean and cooked this familiar dish far from home. Today *coo-coo* is a common food on many Caribbean islands, along with plain maize mush, called *fungee*, which, as in Africa, is eaten with spicy soups and stews.

From its original home in the Americas, maize traveled around the world, influencing the diets and the cooking of many peoples. In northern India, it became a staple crop during the 1800s. Maize was

A woman in modern Kenya grinds maize with stone implements very similar to those used in the ancient Americas.

so common that many Indians believed it had been part of their diet since ancient times. Farmers in southwestern China were growing maize in the 1700s; during the 1800s, maize spread to the north. Today China is second only to the United States in the amount of maize produced each year.

The spread of maize from the New World to the Old made a great contribution to world nutrition, but it also brought with it some problems. The most serious was a strange new disease that seemed to afflict people who ate maize. It caused skin rashes, sore muscles, dizziness, and sometimes even insanity or death.

This disease, first noticed among maize eaters in Italy during the 1700s, was called pellagra, an Italian word meaning "rough skin." By the 1800s, there were epidemics of pellagra in Africa, all in areas where people depended upon maize as a basic food. Some scientists came to believe that the disease was caused by eating maize. But they could not explain why Native Americans had never suffered from pellagra, even though the grain was the most important element in their diet.

The mystery of pellagra was not solved until the early 1900s, when epidemics of the disease began to occur among poor people in the southern United States. Scientists discovered that it was caused by a vitamin deficiency resulting from a diet made up almost completely of maize. One of the reasons that Native Americans had not gotten pellagra was that they usually ate maize along with other foods, particularly beans. Beans, like all legumes, have essential nutrients that maize and other grains lack.

Another thing that prevented pellagra among the native peoples of the Americas was the common method used to prepare maize. As you will remember, cooks in Mexico boiled maize in water containing the mineral lime before grinding it. In North America, wood ash was used for the same purpose. These "alkali treatments" were intended to remove the tough hulls that covered the kernels, but they also improved the nutritional benefits of maize. The minerals released nutrients that maize contained in a form that was otherwise unusable by humans.

The alkali method of preparing maize, plus the American custom of eating the grain along with other foods, prevented any problems of vitamin deficiency. But this preparation method was not transferred to

Europe, Asia, or Africa. And many maize eaters in these areas were so desperately poor that they had no other food. Even in recent times, outbreaks of pellagra have occurred in Africa among people who eat maize mush for every meal.

Today maize is known, if not always loved, in many parts of the world, but it is still very much an American grain. The United States is the leading producer of maize, growing about two-fifths of the world crop. One-half of the U.S. maize crop is used for animal feed, but most of the rest goes into food products.

Just as in earlier times, the people of the Americas eat maize prepared in an amazing variety of ways: as ears fresh from the field; as tortillas,

Maize for sale in a market in Thailand. As in many other parts of the world, the grain will probably be used to feed animals rather than people.

tamales, and *chicha*; as cornflakes and popcorn; as bread and hominy grits. Maize is also consumed in forms that the ancient Native Americans could never have imagined. One is corn oil, made from the oil-rich germ of the maize kernel, which is removed by grinding softened maize with modern milling techniques. Further grinding and processing produces corn starch and corn syrup. These maize products are used in many kinds of prepared foods, including margarine, salad dressing, and baked goods. Today as in the past, maize is on the table almost every time that Americans sit down to eat.

BEANS
New Varieties from a New World

When Columbus said that the "fruits" and "herbage" of the Americas were as different from European plants "as day is from night,"[1] he wasn't too far wrong. Certainly there was nothing back home like the tall maize plant, with its fat kernels enclosed in a husk, or the cacao tree that produced seeds from which Native Americans made a very special drink. Europeans had never before seen a fruit as strange as the sweet, prickly pineapple or a "nut" that grew underground as the American peanut did.

Some of the American foods, however, were not so exotic. In fact, they were very much like foods grown and eaten in Europe. This was certainly true of the beans of the New World. Although American beans eventually came to be widely used in Europe, their initial discovery by Europeans went almost unnoticed. Columbus and other European explorers knew their beans, and they recognized the American varieties as part of a large family of food plants that had been included in the human diet for thousands of years.

Beans, like peas and lentils, belong to a group of plants called legumes. The seeds of these plants, which are enclosed in pods, are among the oldest foods eaten by human beings. Early people gathered legume seeds from wild plants. When humans became farmers, they domesticated these plants and then developed them to produce bigger and better seeds.

In many ancient cultures, common people ate dried lentils cooked in porridges, soups, and stews at almost every meal. (The "mess of pottage" that figures in the Old Testament story about Esau and his birthright is such a dish.) Beans were also on the menu in many parts of the ancient world. In China and other areas of Asia, the soybean was the most important legume, along with varieties such as azuki and mung beans. In Europe, the fava bean, or broad bean, was king.

The people of ancient Greece and Rome ate dried fava beans cooked with garlic and onions. Sometimes they threw the whole young bean pod into the cooking pot. In addition to—or perhaps because of—their importance in the daily diet, fava beans had symbolic meaning. To the Romans, they were connected with the cycle of natural life, representing both the souls of the dead and the new life that comes with birth and with the planting of seeds. The Greeks shared some of these beliefs about the significance of fava beans, but they also had a more practical use for them. Beans served as ballot counters in Greek politics; one bean dropped in a ballot box represented one vote.

Since ancient times, the fava bean was the "Great Garden Bean" in Europe, until the beans of the Americas arrived on the scene.

I *Faba maior hortenſis.*
The great garden Beane.

In Europe during the Middle Ages, fava beans continued to be a basic food for ordinary people. Because beans (and all the other legumes) contain protein, they provided needed nourishment in diets that included little meat. Legumes were even more nutritious when eaten in combination with grains such as wheat, millet, or rice, as they were throughout Europe and Asia. Although beans were important in the diets of millions, they did not have the same significance in this later European world that they had in Roman times. The saying "not worth beans" (or "a hill of beans") originated in the 1300s and indicated the value that Europeans placed on this very basic food.[2]

When Columbus and other explorers set out from Europe in the late 1400s, their ship stores included barrels full of dried legumes. During the long voyages, sailors ate boiled fava beans, lentils, and chickpeas (garbanzos), another common legume in the Mediterranean world. When the European invaders reached the Americas, they found a new world of beans.

The beans of the Americas did not include the familar fava that was so much a part of European diets. The varieties grown in the New World were different, with different origins. Among them were many of the beans known around the world today—kidney, green, black, navy, pinto, wax, and lima. All these bean varieties are part of a single scientific genus called *Phaseolus*, and many were developed by Native American farmers centuries ago.

Just as in Europe and Asia, beans were among the earliest plants to be domesticated in the Americas. Evidence of this early cultivation has been found in archaeological excavations in South America and in Mexico. Seeds and pods of lima beans and of varieties of the so-called common bean appear as early as 6000 B.C.

Lima beans, which make up one of the four American species of *Phaseolus*, got their modern name from Lima, the capital of the Spanish colony in Peru. Established in 1535, the city had existed for a much shorter time than the beans named after it. Seeds and pods of lima beans are often found preserved in the ruins of ancient Peruvian houses and villages. Other evidence of the lima bean's importance in this area can be found on pieces of pottery. The Moche people, who lived in the coastal region of Peru from about A.D. 100 to 800, painted images of lima beans on pottery vessels.

Some of these images show human runners carrying small bags that are decorated with pictures of lima beans. Archaeologists are not sure what such scenes mean. Did the Moche use lima beans in some kind of communication system, with runners delivering messages somehow "coded" in beans? Or do the scenes on the pots picture some religious ceremony involving beans?

Other Moche images of lima beans are equally mysterious. Some show figures with human heads and limbs attached to lima-bean bodies. Armed with spears and shields, these tiny lima-bean "warriors" are engaged in fierce battles. The significance of these pictures is not known, but one thing is clear: For the Moche as for the ancient Romans, beans had a symbolic meaning in addition to their importance as food.

Lima beans were popular in ancient Peru, but the bean that dominated most of the Americas was the common bean (*Phaseolus vulgaris*). This species of *Phaseolus* includes the varieties best

A pottery vessel made by the Moche people of Peru shows figures with human heads and lima-bean bodies engaged in battle.

known today, including kidney, green, wax, and pinto beans. Not all of these varieties were found in the ancient Americas, but the common bean in some form was everywhere. Along with maize, squash, and capsicum peppers, it was a basic food in the diets of people in Mexico and in many parts of North and South America. (In South America, potatoes and the starchy root manioc also played major roles.)

Among the Aztecs, common beans were so important that they were included in the tribute collected by the central government. Each year, every province in the Aztec state had to contribute about eight thousand bushels of dried beans and the same amount of maize and several other grains. Friar Bernardino de Sahagún tells us that the Aztecs had twelve different kinds of beans; among them were black beans, "big, long and flat," and red beans, "chili-red, blood colored." Sahagún describes the preparation of another variety, the yellow bean: "It can be cooked in an olla [a clay pot]; it can be baked. It is tasty, savory, pleasing, very pleasing. . . . Grains of maize can be added."[3]

Native American cooks often combined beans with maize. In the great Aztec marketplace, Friar Sahagún reports that maize tortillas were sold with

A bean seller in the Aztec marketplace, as pictured in the Florentine Codex. The scroll-like elements at the top, known as "speech-curls," were used by native artists to indicate that the person in the picture was talking.

"shelled beans, cooked shelled beans, uncooked shelled beans; with shelled beans mashed."[4] In North America, a dish called *m'sickqquatasch* in the Narraganset language was made of dried beans boiled with fresh kernels of maize. Today this dish is called succotash and is usually made with lima beans instead of some variety of the common bean originally used by native cooks in North America.

The combination of beans and maize made both foods more nutritious, just as combining beans with rice or wheat improved the diets of people in Europe and Asia. Native Americans not only ate beans and maize together but also grew the two plants in the same fields. In many parts of the Americas, beans were planted right next to maize so that their climbing vines could use the sturdy maize stalks as support.

The people of the Americas ate some maize when it was green and fresh, but beans were usually dried and stored for future use. At the time of harvest, the seeds were removed from the bean pods and spread out to dry in the sun. In North America, native farmers sometimes dried whole beans, pod and all, producing what European settlers called "leatherbritches beans." After the dried beans were cooked, the leathery pods were removed from the pot and the seeds alone were eaten.[5]

The common bean, with its many varieties, and the lima bean were the most widely grown legumes in the Americas, but two other species of *Phaseolus* could also be found in native gardens. One was the scarlet runner bean, a plant with beautiful red flowers that was grown in cooler regions of Mexico. The fourth American bean was the tepary, a tough plant adapted to arid regions of Mexico and the southern part of North America. The tepary was the only one of the American beans that did not leave the land of its origins. All the others were introduced into the Old World and quickly became great successes in their new homes.

American beans arrived in Europe soon after Europeans first set foot in the New World. Columbus probably brought bean seeds back to Spain after his second voyage in 1493. By the 1540s, the new beans began appearing in herbals published in Europe, although their American origins seemed to be unknown.

Smilax hortensis.
Roomsche Boonen.

One of the earliest European drawings of American beans, from Leonhart Fuchs's herbal, 1543. Because they were vining plants, the New World beans were at first thought to be a kind of smilax, a clinging garden vine.

In England, the scarlet runner bean quickly became popular, but not as a source of food. Instead, the climbing vine with its brilliant red flowers was grown as an ornamental plant. In the late 1500s, John Gerard, the author of the famous early herbal, had scarlet runner beans growing on tall poles in his garden at Holborn in London. The American bean plant was nicknamed the "painted lady" because of its elegant scarlet blooms.

It was not long before Europeans discovered that the New World beans could fill their stomachs as well as delight their eyes. As farmers and gardeners became familiar with the dozens of varieties of American beans, they began to grow them in place of the old, familiar fava, which John Gerard called the "Great Garden Bean." The new beans were very easy to grow, and they had some advantages over the fava, including a thinner seed coat that did not have to be removed before eating.

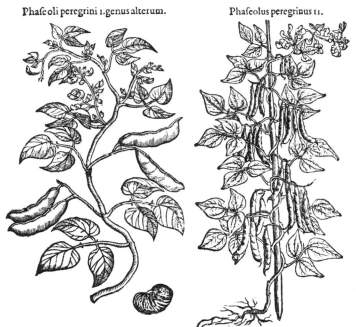

Phafeoli peregrini 1.genus alterum.   Phafeolus peregrinus 11.

In an herbal by Charles L'Ecluse published in 1601, the beans of the Americas are called by the scientific name *Phaseolus*, which is still used today.

For some Europeans, eating American beans proved healthier than eating fava beans. People from Greece and other Mediterranean countries who ate favas or even inhaled pollen from the plants sometimes developed an allergic reaction called favism. Caused by an inherited enzyme deficiency, favism had some serious symptoms, including anemia and jaundice. New World beans did not produce this reaction.

New World beans did produce a less dangerous symptom, flatulence, which was also caused by their Old World relatives. In the 1500s, this physical condition was often referred to as "windiness." Today we commonly call it gas. It is caused by the activity of bacteria in the human digestive system working on the complex sugars contained in beans. Other foods such as lentils, broccoli, cabbage, and even raisins contain these sugars and can produce the same "gassy" symptoms, but beans have always been the biggest culprit for most people.[6]

The familiar problem of "windiness" did not discourage Europeans of the 1500s from eating American beans. In a very short time after their introduction, the new varieties became an important part of European cooking. Soon they were being used in dishes that are today considered typical of European national cuisines. In Italy, for example, white kidney beans, known as *cannellini*, became an essential ingredient in the thick vegetable soup minestrone. Southern Italian cooks also combined *cannellini* with pasta and tomatoes to make a hearty dish called *pasta e fagioli* (pasta and beans). Italian immigrants brought this bean dish with them to the United States, where it was often known as *pasta fazool*, a name in a dialect spoken in southern Italy.

Cooks in France fell in love with the New World beans and did all kinds of inventive things with them. The French

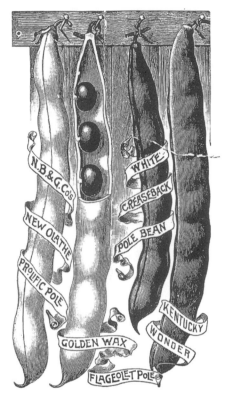

The flageolet is a variety of the American common bean developed in France during the 1700s.

called the new beans *haricots*, a word that may be derived from the Aztec word for beans, *ayocotl*. In southern France, *haricots blancs* (the same white kidney beans popular in Italy) were combined with various kinds of meats to create cassoulet, a savory dish known today as a French speciality. Bean eaters in France also enjoyed fresh whole beans, cooked pod and all. These *haricots verts*, or green beans, became one of the most popular modern ways of serving beans. French farmers even developed new varieties of the American beans, for example, the flageolet, a bean with pale green seeds that were removed from the pod when young and eaten fresh.

BEANS

The French became so closely associated with bean cookery that other countries adopted bean names from French cuisine. Today in England, dried beans are usually known as haricots, while beans eaten fresh and whole are called French beans. In the United States as well, green beans are sometimes referred to as French-style or French-cut. Thanks to the complicated twists of history, these beans native to the Americas have been given a French pedigree.

The New World beans had their biggest success in Europe, where they suited local climates and diets. They did not catch on as well in Asia. In Asian countries such as India and China, lentils, soybeans, azuki beans, and mung beans continued to reign supreme. Some American beans, particularly limas, found a place in the cooking of Africa. Africa also contributed a legume to the regional cooking of North America. Black slaves transported to American plantations brought with them the native African cowpea, or black-eyed pea (actually a kind of bean). In the American South, black-eyed peas were

Beans from the Americas grow in this garden in Burundi, Africa, along with another American plant, manioc. In the background are banana trees, which are native to the Old World.

combined with rice and ham or pork to make a dish called Hoppin' John, which was traditionally eaten on New Year's Day to bring good luck.

Just like maize and potatoes, American beans stayed at home at the same time that they traveled around the world. In modern Mexico, many people eat beans every day, just as they did in the time of the Maya and Aztecs. *Frijoles de olla*, black beans or pinto beans cooked for hours in a big clay pot, are a part of most meals, usually served after the main course and before dessert. *Frijoles refritos* (refried beans), a Mexican bean dish that often appears on restaurant menus in North America, has a mixed American and European ancestry. It is made of boiled pinto beans mashed and cooked with lard, a fat from the pigs that Europeans introduced to the Americas.

Beans are also popular in the Caribbean, where almost every island has its own special way of preparing and serving them. Most of these dishes combine beans with rice to make a nourishing and filling meal. In Jamaica, red kidney beans and rice are cooked in rich, fragrant coconut milk. Cubans combine pork or ham with black beans and rice in a dish commonly called *Moros y Cristianos*. This name, which refers to the dish's blend of black and white, comes from the island's Spanish heritage. It recalls the period in Spanish history when the dark-skinned Moors, Muslim people from North Africa, ruled the Christian inhabitants of Spain.

In North America, green beans are probably the most popular bean dish, but bean soup and succotash still appear on family dinner tables. American picnics would not be complete without a pan of sweet, savory baked beans. This dish had its beginnings as a Native American specialty, beans mixed with maple syrup and bear fat and cooked in "bean holes" lined with hot rocks. European colonists substituted molasses or sugar for the maple syrup and bacon or ham for the bear fat. They cooked their beans in pots set in the coals of a fire rather than in underground bean holes, but the results were the same.

Today most people think of beans as a simple, ordinary food, but in at least one part of modern North America, they are treated with the same respect that they received in ancient times. The Hopi Indians of the southwestern United States grow beans in their small gardens carved out of the desert. Each year, early in spring, they celebrate a bean festival called Powamu.

In preparation for the festival, bean seeds are planted in boxes of moist sand and kept in a warm place until they sprout. When Powamu begins, masked kachina dancers representing powerful spirits of nature bless

This advertisement from an old seed catalog shows the wax bean, a variety of the common bean developed in the 1830s to be eaten whole and fresh.

the long, pale green bean sprouts. Later they distribute the sprouts to the people in the Hopi villages, who cook them in stews eaten at the end of Powamu to ensure that the bean crop will thrive during the coming year.

The Hopi, like people in many other parts of the world, make beans part of their daily diet. Whether baked or boiled, mashed or fried, wrapped in tamales or mixed with rice, beans fill the stomach and satisfy the appetite. Thanks to the beans that originated in the Americas, the world menu now includes many more varieties of this basic food.

PEPPERS
Hot and Sweet

On January 15, 1493, Christopher Columbus recorded in his journal that he had found much "*aji*" on the Caribbean island of Hispaniola. He called *aji* the "pepper" of the native people, comparing it to the precious black seasoning so prized in Europe, and noted, "No one eats without it because it is very healthy."[1]

Twenty-six years later, Spanish conquistadores in Mexico discovered that a pungent food plant called *chilli* was a very important part of Aztec cuisine. The Aztecs grew many varieties, including "mild red chillies, broad chillies, hot green chillies, yellow chillies, . . . water chillies, . . . tree chillies."[2]

Aji (pronounced AH-hee) and *chilli* are two different Native American names for one very important plant. This plant and the food products made from it became one of the most popular exports from the New World to the Old, and one of

The *chilli* seller bargains with a customer in the Aztec marketplace.

the most overlooked. Today the plant is grown around the world and is still known by a variety of confusing and contradictory names. For example, among English-speaking people, it may be called hot pepper, sweet pepper, green pepper, chili pepper, chilli, chile, capsicum, cayenne, or paprika.

Its common names may be confusing, but the plant is no mystery to botanists. It is a member of the family Solanaceae, which includes other familiar American natives such as potatoes, tomatoes, and tobacco. It makes up a genus called *Capsicum*, a term that comes from a Latin word for box. This name probably refers to the vaguely boxlike shape of the plant's fruits, the parts that contain the seeds. Capsicum fruits are hollow, fleshy-walled capsules with many seeds inside. Most are green in their immature stage and some shade of yellow or red when ripe.

Botanists recognize only four separate species within the genus *Capsicum*, but these few species include dozens of different varieties. Some varieties have large, juicy fruits with a mild taste. The fruits of others are tiny and fiery hot, causing a burning sensation in the mouth. Because of this effect, capsicums have often been confused with the plant that produces black pepper, another pungent food product. In fact, there is no botanical relationship between the two kinds of plants.

Black pepper comes from the berries of a vining plant in the genus *Piper*. Native to India, varieties of this plant have been cultivated by humans for thousands of years. In ancient times pepper, as well as spices such as cinnamon, nutmeg, and ginger, were traded along land and sea routes that led from India to Greece, Italy, and other countries around the Mediterranean Sea. Pepper was the most precious and valued of the spices to reach the Western world. Used to season and preserve food, peppercorns, the dried berries of the pepper plant, were often worth their weight in gold. In medieval Europe, pepper was even used as a medium of exchange, with rents and taxes paid in this precious spice.

Black pepper, the precious spice that Europeans could not get enough of. (From Charles L'Ecluse's herbal)

For many centuries, the European spice trade was dominated by merchants from Arab nations. These skilled traders brought ships from India and other spice-growing countries of the East and then carried the goods overland to ports on the Mediterranean Sea. By the mid-1400s, another Muslim power, the Ottoman Turks, controlled the land and sea routes to the riches of the East. European nations were eager to find new ways to reach India and the spice islands of the East Indies.

The search for spices, as well as for gold, inspired many voyages of exploration during the late 1400s. In the 1480s, Portuguese explorers discovered that by sailing south around the tip of Africa, they could enter the Indian Ocean. By 1498, Vasco da Gama had proved that it was possible to travel by sea from Europe to the fabulous spice lands of the East.

Six years earlier, Christopher Columbus had tried another approach. Sailing under the flag of Spain, the Italian mariner headed west rather than south in the hope of circling the globe and reaching the East Indies. When he stumbled instead on the islands of a new world, he searched eagerly for

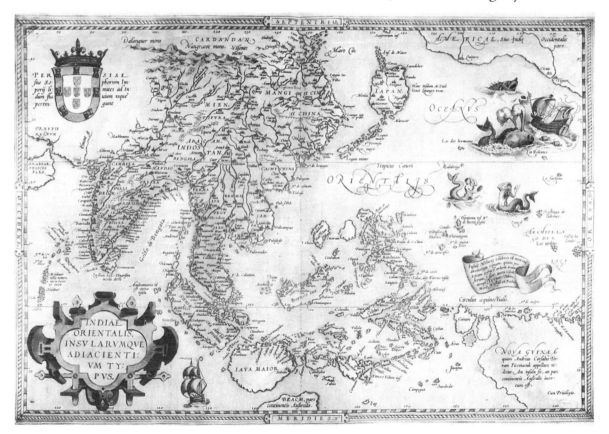

A map of the East Indies from the first modern atlas, published in Antwerp in 1570. The search for pepper and other spices brought European explorers to this distant part of the world.

spice-bearing plants, including the vine that produced the black pepper so valued in Europe. Instead, he found a completely new plant, *aji*, one of the varieties of the capsicums. The fruits of this plant and the products made from them would add more fire to the world diet than pepper ever did.

Black pepper did not grow in the Americas, but the capsicums were common cultivated plants in many areas. They had been developed from a small wild plant that was native to tropical regions of South America. Capsicums may have been domesticated as early as 7000 B.C. By the time that Europeans arrived in the 1500s, many of the varieties known today were growing in the gardens of Native American farmers on the Caribbean Islands, in Mexico, and in the warmer regions of South and North America.

Aji was the name for the plant used by the Arawak people of the Caribbean, and it was the name that Europeans probably first heard. But most Europeans, like Columbus, immediately associated the spicy capsicums with pepper. When Columbus found *aji* on Hispaniola, he speculated that it could be worth more than "our pepper" (*pimienta* in Spanish). The explorer even dreamed of sending fifty shiploads of *aji* from Hispaniola to Europe each year.[3]

Michele de Cuneo, an Italian who accompanied Columbus on his second voyage to the Americas in 1493, recorded some more practical information on the plant: "In those islands there are also bushes like rose bushes which make a fruit . . . full of small grains as biting as pepper; those Caribs and the Indians eat that fruit as we eat apples."[4]

Cuneo's observation about this strange new plant was accurate. The "biting" parts of a capsicum fruit are, in fact, the seeds ("small grains") and the parts surrounding them inside the capsule. They contain chemical compounds called capsaicins, which cause a burning sensation in the mouth and throat. The rest of the fruit, according to Bartolome de las Casas, a later Spanish observer, "is not pungent; it is sweet and smooth."[5]

The native peoples of the Caribbean ate *aji* fresh from the plant—"as we eat apples"—and also used them in cooked dishes. In Mexico, the Aztecs developed many ways of preparing *chillies*, the name for capsicums in Nahuatl, the Aztec language. In his account of Aztec life, the Spanish friar Bernardino de Sahagún reported some of the dishes that included these versatile food plants. Among them were "turkey with a sauce of small chillies, tomatoes, and ground squash seeds; . . . sauces of ordinary tomatoes . . . and yellow chilli, or of tomatoes and green chilli; . . . white fish with yellow chilli; grey fish with red chilli, tomatoes, and ground squash seeds."[6]

As this list suggests, Aztec cooks often combined fresh chillies with tomatoes to make spicy sauces that, according to Friar Sahagún, were "hot, very hot, very glistening-hot."[7] They also used capsicums in the form of a powder made by grinding the dried fruits of the plant. This powder could be sprinkled on fresh foods or added to cooked dishes. Mixed with ground cacao seeds and water, it made a spicy, highly regarded drink. Whether they were cooked, eaten fresh, or used as a seasoning, the American peppers were a vital part of the Native American diet.

Like Columbus, many European explorers were impressed by the seasoning power of the capsicums. They brought specimens of the plants home with them during the 1500s, but the new "peppers" were not quickly accepted in European countries. Many considered their heat *too* powerful. In an herbal published in 1554, Rembert Dodoens, a Flemish doctor, warned that this new plant "killeth dogs, if it be given them to eat."[8] If Europeans grew capsicums at all in this period, they grew them mainly as ornamental plants. They were not used widely as food until much later, when the sweet varieties became popular.

Although not well received in Europe, the hot American peppers were wildly successful in Asia and Africa. Large parts of these continents had climates suitable for growing plants that had come from tropical America. More importantly, people in many of these areas already ate highly seasoned foods. When the capsicums arrived in Asia and Africa, they became so popular that they replaced some of the spices that had been used for centuries to add fire to food.

Portuguese traders were largely responsible for bringing capsicums to these distant parts of the world. Through their explorations in the 1400s, the Portuguese had gained footholds on both the west and the east coasts of Africa. Portuguese voyages to India and the East Indies had created new trade routes that brought spices and other exotic goods from the East. Explorers from Portugal reached the Americas in the early 1500s, and by 1530, Portuguese colonies were established in Brazil.

With their far-flung trade network, the Portuguese brought together people and goods from all over the world. One of the small but important items they traded was the fiery capsicum. Portuguese ships carried this American food plant to the west coast of Africa, where cooks already used a hot spice that was sometimes called pepper. This was not the precious black pepper from India but a member of the ginger family known as malagueta pepper, or "grain of paradise." When the capsicums reached Africa, they took the place of this seasoning in spicy stews and sauces.

By the early 1500s, the American peppers were grown and eaten in many parts of Africa south of the Sahara Desert. By the 1540s, several kinds of capsicums could be found growing in India. As in Africa, they had been brought by traders from Portugal. From the Portuguese port of Goa on the southwestern coast, the spicy capsicums quickly made their way to all parts of India where "hot" foods were eaten. Along with traditional Indian spices such as ginger, cumin, turmeric, and coriander, they soon became a vital part of the seasonings used in these regions.

Thanks largely to the Portuguese, the capsicums also reached China in the early 1500s. Parts of this vast country, particularly the southwestern regions of Yunnan and Szechwan, had a long tradition of spicy foods. For centuries, cooks in these regions had used a seasoning called *fagara*, known to Europeans as brown or Szechwan pepper. Made from the berries of an ash

Capsicon rubeum & nigrum.
Peper van Jndien.

Capsicon oblongius.
Lange Peper van Jndien.

When Leonhart Fuchs pictured capsicum peppers in his 1543 herbal, he described them as "pepper from India."

tree, *fagara* gave a spicy savor to food but nothing to equal the fire of the capsicums. The American peppers were very welcome here.

The capsicums traveled to Africa, India, and other Eastern countries with great speed and almost immediately became part of the local styles of cooking. This transfer happened so quickly that many people were convinced the plants had always been grown and eaten in these areas.

When capsicums began appearing in European herbals during the mid-1500s, they were often given names based on these supposed Eastern origins. In 1543, Leonhart Fuchs, the author of one of the earliest herbals, described

3 *Capsicum minimis siliquis.*
Small codded Ginny Pepper.

‡ *Capsici siliquæ varia.*
Varieties of the cods of Ginny pepper.

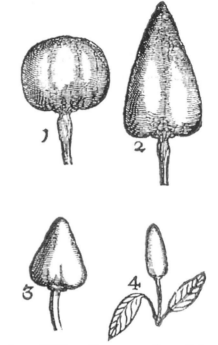

Varieties of "Ginny" peppers from John Gerard's herbal

them as Indian or Calicut peppers (Calicut was the port where the Portuguese had first landed in India). The English herbalist John Gerard later referred to the capsicums as "Ginny" peppers after the country of Guinea in West Africa.

Although these names were inaccurate, they did reveal something about the way that the capsicums became known in parts of Europe. They were not introduced directly from the Americas but came by way of the East. This was what happened in the Balkan region, the location of modern Hungary, Romania, Yugoslavia, Bosnia, and Croatia. During the 1500s and 1600s, this whole area was controlled by the Ottoman Turks, who had discovered spicy capsicums in India and other parts of the East. The Turks introduced them into their vast empire, and they were enthusiastically received.

In Hungary, the American peppers were called paprika, a name derived from the local word for black pepper. Most popular were the mildly spicy red varieties, which were dried and ground into a savory powder. This form of paprika, used to season stews and goulashes, became one of the characteristic ingredients of Hungarian cooking.

In other parts of Europe, the capsicums came to be used mainly as fresh vegetables rather than as a seasoning. In Italy and Spain, sweet green and red peppers (nonspicy varieties of capsicums) were cooked in olive oil and combined with tomatoes and onions to make delectable sauces. Spanish cooks also roasted red peppers and marinated them in olive oil, creating the food known today in the United States as pimento. Another way of preparing sweet peppers in the Mediterranean world was stuffing them with a mixture of rice and meat.

It was in Africa and Asia, however, that cooks came to use capsicums in the most varied and imaginative ways. Today the cooking in large parts of these continents still depends on the spicy American peppers.

PEPPER.

Sow the seeds early under glass, or in the open ground in warm weather; transplant when three inches high.

Pepper, Ruby King, a handsome and very productive variety; fruit 4½ to 6 inches long by 3½ to 4 inches broad. When ripe they are bright ruby-red; remarkably mild and pleasant. Per oz., 40 cents; ½ ounce, 25 cents............................... 5

Golden Dawn, a new variety, resembling the Large Bell in shape, but more delicate in flavor, and the color is a rich, golden yellow; per oz., 30 cents; ½ oz., 20 cents 5

Large Bell, very large—nearly four inches long and three inches in diameter; glossy red; per oz., 30 cents; ½ oz., 20 cents 5

Sweet Mountain, or Mammoth, much like Bell, perhaps a little larger; per oz., 30 cents; ¼ oz., 20 cents................. 5

Monstrous, or Grossum, a French variety, the largest we have ever grown; per oz., 30 c.; ½ oz., 20 cents 5

SWEET MOUNTAIN, OR MAMMOTH.

Peppers listed in a seed catalog from 1891. Most are the sweet, mild varieties preferred by American gardeners.

A young man sells peppers at a market in Senegal, West Africa.

In Africa, many countries use special sauces and spice mixtures that are based on hot peppers. The people of Mozambique make a fiery sauce called *piripiri* out of lemon juice and small red peppers originally brought by the Portuguese from Brazil. This sauce is used to marinate seafood and to liven up many meat and vegetable dishes. Ethiopians make *berebere*, a dry mixture of ground peppers and other spices such as ginger and cloves. In addition to these seasonings, African cooks use hot capsicums, both fresh and dry, as an ingredient in stews, soups, and many other dishes.

In India, capsicums are used in a variety of subtle ways, most often in making curries. Indian cooking includes many kinds of curries, each with its own special combination of spices. There is no such thing as ready-made curry powder in India. To prepare a hot curry dish, a cook first grinds dried peppers along with other whole spices such as cumin and coriander. Then the spices are mixed with water or oil and cooked for a while to blend the different flavors. Meats, vegetables, and other ingredients such as coconut milk are added to the cooked spice mixture, often along with fresh peppers or yet another blend of spices.

Indians also use fresh capsicums in chutneys, sweet or tangy relishes that accompany meals. Chutneys can be made with fruits, vegetables, vinegar, sugar, and a great variety of other ingredients, but they often include a few hot peppers.

Other Asian countries have their own ways of using the hot American peppers. In Indonesia, relishes called *sambals* rival the chutneys of India in adding a spicy tang to a meal. Cooks in Thailand grind capsicums with other spices to make fiery pastes that are stirred into hot oil and used in currylike dishes.

Chinese food from the Szechwan and Yunnan regions combines fresh and dried capsicums with meat and vegetables in spicy stir-fried dishes. Kung Pao chicken, for example, is a Szechwan specialty that uses hot American peppers along with cashews, nuts native to South America. Peanuts, also from the Americas, are another ingredient found in spicy Chinese dishes.

Capsicums, of course, have remained an important cooking ingredient in the American lands of their origins. Today in Mexico, they are called *chiles*, the Spanish version of the Nahuatl *chilli*. Varieties such as the poblano, the serrano, and the jalapeño appear in stews and sauces along with tomatoes and in other dishes very similar to the ones the Aztecs prepared centuries ago. On the islands of the West Indies, *aji* is still an important ingredient in sauces, thanks in part to the heritage of African cooking brought by slaves.

Until recently, spicy capsicums were not very popular in most parts of North America. Sweet peppers were widely used as an ingredient in salads or sometimes stuffed with rice and meat. American cooks also liked the mildly spicy paprika, adding it to dishes not so much for its flavor but for a dash of color.

Another savory seasoning usually found in American kitchens was chili powder, a blend of ground dried capsicums and several other spices, including oregano, cumin, and garlic. Chili powder was invented in the late 1800s to use in chili con carne, a dish that originated not in Mexico, but in the southwestern United States. Originally a combination of chunks of meat and fresh capsicums, chili con carne is now made with ground beef, beans, tomatoes, and many other ingredients.

Other than chili powder and paprika, cooks in most parts of North

Since 1868, Americans have been spicing up their food with Tabasco, a hot pepper sauce made by the McIlhenny family of Avery, Louisiana.

America for many years had little interest in spicy seasonings and ingredients. But some regions had a long tradition of preparing and eating "hot" foods. In the southwestern United States, which used to be part of Mexico, cooks have used fresh hot chiles ever since the 1700s. This is also true in New Orleans and other centers of Creole cooking, which combines African, French, and Spanish influences.

In recent years, however, the use of spicy capsicums has become much more widespread. Mexican and southwestern dishes now appear on restaurant menus all over the United States. Salsa, which combines tomatoes with fresh hot peppers, has become almost as popular as ketchup. Today supermarkets in St. Paul and Seattle as well as Sante Fe and San Antonio often have fresh jalapeño and serrano peppers in their produce departments.

Immigrants to the United States from Mexico and from Asian countries such as Vietnam and Thailand have also helped to focus more attention on spicy capsicums. Today thousands of North Americans are discovering the many varieties of the American peppers and the hundreds of ways that they

can be used to add spice to food. They are learning a lesson in cooking that the rest of the world learned more than three centuries ago.

A modern spice blend (left) combines black pepper with capsicum peppers, for "those who prefer a peppier pepper."

PEANUTS

From the Americas
to Africa and Back Again

If ever there was a food that seems typically "American," it is the peanut. In the United States, roasted peanuts, in or out of the shell, are traditionally eaten at ball games, circuses, and zoos. Today they are also a tradition on airplanes, where passengers usually get packets of dry-roasted peanuts to munch on during the flight. Peanut butter is the favorite food of millions of American children. And peanuts even have a place in American history. During the Civil War, the most serious conflict ever to divide the United States, soldiers from both the North and the South ate peanuts and even sang a song about them.

Peanuts *are* a truly American food. They had their origins in the Americas and today are a cherished part of American life. But peanuts have also had a long history in Africa and Asia, where they have had an even more important role to play.

South America is where the peanut got its start, more than three thousand years ago. The people of ancient Peru domesticated wild peanut plants and raised crops of peanuts in the sandy soil of the dry coastal regions. Archaeological excavations suggest that peanuts must have been a common food in these areas. Thousands of peanut shells, preserved by the dry climate, have been found at many sites, dating back to at least 2500 B.C.

Other clues that peanuts were important in ancient Peru have been discovered in burials of the Moche people, who lived in the region from about A.D. 100 to 800. Among the precious items enclosed in Moche graves were pottery vessels decorated with three-dimensional images of peanut shells. In a later period, Inca burials often included small string bags containing peanuts, maize, beans, and peppers, plants that were considered important in this world and the next.

This jar decorated with peanuts was made by the Moche people of ancient Peru. It is a type of vessel known as a stirrup jar because of the stirrup-shaped spout on top.

From their place of origin in South America, peanuts spread to Mexico some time before 500 B.C. The Aztecs grew peanuts but did not make them an important part of their diet. In fact, they seemed to have considered them more a medicine than a food. Friar Sahagún tells us that in the Aztec marketplace, peanuts were sold by the "medicine seller," who was "a knower of herbs, a knower of roots, a physician."[1] Ground and mixed with water, peanuts were used as a remedy for fever.

Peanuts were also cultivated on the islands of the Caribbean, where they were an important food item. A Spanish account from 1535 mentions a plant called *mani* grown by the people of Hispaniola: "They sow and harvest it. It is a very common crop . . . about the size of a pine nut in the shell. They consider it a healthy food."[2]

When the Spanish and Portuguese invaded South America in the early 1500s, they found peanuts growing in Peru, Brazil, and other regions. Here the American nuts were known by names such as *mandubi* and *mandi*. Even though Europeans noted that the native people ate peanuts, they themselves were cautious. Bernabe Cobo, a Catholic priest who lived in Peru during the early 1600s, claimed that consuming peanuts caused ailments such as headaches and dizziness. Some Europeans in South America thought that peanuts might be used as a substitute for almonds or roasted and ground to made a kind of coffee. Few, however, were enthusiastic about this new food.[3]

Drawings of peanut leaves, shells, and kernels from a book about Brazil published in 1658

53

One reason for this cool reaction may have been the strangeness of the peanut plant to European eyes. With its kernels enclosed inside a hard shell, the peanut seemed to be similar to nuts of the Old World such as the hazelnut and the almond. But these familiar nuts came from trees, whereas the American "nut" grew underground at the base of a small, bushy plant.

In fact, peanuts have nothing in common, botanically speaking, with the nuts of the Old World or American nuts such as the pecan. Instead, they are legumes, closely related to beans, peas, and lentils. But even within the legume family, the peanut is an oddity. The plant looks something like a pea plant, but its method of growth is very different.

The peanut is a legume, like beans and peas, but its pods develop underground.

Like peas and many other kinds of food plants, peanuts reproduce by means of flowers. Peanut flowers grow on the lower branches of the plant. After the flowers are pollinated and fertilized, the developing ovaries (which will become the peanut pods) begin to reach downward, toward the ground. They form "pegs" that push their way two or three inches beneath the soil. Here the pods continue their development, with the seeds, or kernels, forming inside. Peanuts are harvested by digging up the whole plant, with the mature pods still attached.

Europeans who first encountered peanuts in the 1500s found them strangely different from the nuts they knew at home. Although the Spanish and Portuguese probably took the plants back to Europe, they were not widely cultivated there. (The climate in much of Europe was not really warm enough for growing peanuts.) Instead, like the capsicum peppers, peanuts found a new home in Africa and Asia.

Like peppers, peanuts were first brought to Africa by Portuguese merchants and seamen. During the 1560s, they were already growing on the continent's west coast, in the same areas where Portuguese and other European slave traders were doing their deadly business. The Portuguese also introduced peanuts into southern India, but Spain was probably responsible for bringing them to the rest of Asia.

In the late 1500s, Spanish colonies in the Americas were connected by trade routes to the Spanish-controlled islands of the Philippines. Fleets of galleons sailed from Mexico's west coast thousands of miles across the Pacific Ocean to the great port of Manila. The Manila galleons brought products from the New World and silver from Mexican mines, which was used to buy silks, spices, porcelain, and other exotic goods from the East. On the return trip, this precious cargo was unloaded at the port of Acapulco, where European traders were waiting to bargain for it.[1] Along with many other New World goods, peanuts traveled along this route, spreading from the Philippines to China, Japan, and the East Indies. Once the American legumes reached these distant places, they quickly took root.

In Africa, peanuts filled a real need, just like maize and manioc (another American plant food). Although the continent was vast and varied in its climate and geography, it had few native plants suitable for cultivation. Peanuts were particularly welcome because they were not only easy to grow but also provided badly needed nourishment. The legumes are 26 percent protein and contain a healthy supply of vegetable oil. When peanuts arrived in Africa in the 1500s, they were a valuable addition to the diets of people who ate very little meat.

In West Africa, peanuts quickly became an important ingredient in everyday cooking, not just a snack food as they would become later in North America. Roasted peanuts were ground and then mixed with green, leafy vegetables. Ground peanuts were also stirred into thick soups and stews made with yams, tomatoes, okra, and other vegetables.

Today, many nations and tribal groups in modern West Africa have their own special recipes for "groundnut" stew (the name for peanuts in parts of Africa where English is spoken). In Ghana, it is known as *nkatekwan* and is usually served with *fufu*, dumplings made out of cooked and mashed manioc, yams, or plantains (a kind of banana). The Bombara people in Mali and Senegal make a version of peanut stew called *mafe*, which includes such delicious ingredients as chicken, okra, tomatoes, and sweet potatoes.

When peanuts arrived in Asia, they quickly became part of everyday food, just as in Africa. Cooks in Southeast Asia discovered that ground peanuts made great sauces for rice, meats, and vegetables. They created many spicy mixtures that combined peanuts with hot capsicum peppers, coconut milk, lime juice, and a variety of other ingredients. Today in Indonesia and Thailand, peanut sauces are always served with the popular snack food *satay*, pieces of tender meat grilled on skewers.

The peanut is put to very good use in modern Indonesia, a country made up of many islands and many different cultures. Tangy peanut sauce tops a salad of cooked vegetables called *gado gado*, which is served throughout the country. Fried peanut fritters made of ground peanuts and rice flour are popular on the island of Java. At special occasions on Java, a festive rice dish is served sprinkled with peanuts combined with toasted coconut and spices.

When peanuts were introduced to China and India in the 1500s, they

The American peanut became a popular food in many parts of Asia. This farmer in modern Burma is roasting peanuts over a fire.

quickly became a part of traditional dishes that had been made for centuries. Cooks in southern India added ground peanuts to curry sauces and garnished curry dishes with whole peanuts. In the Szechwan and Yunnan regions of China, peanuts joined capsicum peppers as ingredients in fiery stir-fried dishes.

In both Asia and Africa, peanuts were valued not just for the rich, nutty taste they added to dishes but also because of their wonderful oil. When peanuts are crushed, they produce a clear oil that can be used for cooking. Cooks in Africa and Asia were very impressed by the quality of peanut oil. It was almost tasteless so it didn't add any new flavor to food (as olive oil does). Even better, it could be heated to a high temperature without smoking or burning. This was very important in preparing foods by deep-fat-frying or stir-frying, which were common methods used by African and Asian cooks.

Peanut oil quickly became the most important cooking oil used in many parts of Africa and Asia, and it remains so today. Cooks in Europe also discovered the impressive qualities of peanut oil. Although peanuts never became popular as a cooking ingredient or a snack food in Europe, peanut oil came to be widely used. This was especially true in France, where today famous chefs cook their elaborate dishes in oil made from the humble American peanut.

Peanut oil, peanut sauce, peanut stew, peanut fritters: These are just some of the ways that the American "nut" came to be used in cooking around the world. For many years in North America, however, peanuts were not considered an acceptable food by most people. They were fare only for animals or for those who did the work of animals. The story of the peanut in North America is closely connected with the painful story of slavery.

Beginning in the late 1500s, white Europeans took black people from Africa and forced them to work on plantations in the Americas. In Brazil and the islands of the Caribbean, sugar was the crop raised by means of slave labor. During the colonial period in North America, African slaves worked on tobacco, rice, and indigo plantations. Later, cotton became the most important plantation crop, especially in the South. During the 1700s and 1800s, thousands of Africans were kidnapped from their homes by slave traders and transported to the United States to do the backbreaking labor required to raise cotton.

Most of the black slaves brought to North America came from the west coast of Africa. This was the area where the Portuguese had first introduced the American peanut in the 1500s and where it had become an important food. When West Africans were enslaved and taken in chains to the United States, the peanut came with them. In fact, peanuts (as well as dried maize) were sometimes used to feed slaves during the long and terrible voyage across the Atlantic.

At this fort on the coast of West Africa, European slave traders loaded African captives onto ships bound for the Americas. Along with the slaves came the American peanut.

Before this time, a few native people in North America had grown peanuts, and early European settlers had used them as animal feed. But during the 1700s and 1800s, the peanut began to take on a new importance in the United States. African slaves continued to grow and eat peanuts just as they had back home. They used them to add variety and nourishment to the diet of beans, corn bread, and greens provided by southern plantation owners. Whites raised peanuts to feed to their cows and pigs, but they still did not consider them suitable food for humans. (Slaves, of course, did not fall into this category.)

This white attitude toward peanuts began to change in the 1860s, during the Civil War. Food shortages in the South made even the despised "goober peas" seem like a desirable food. (This southern name for peanuts probably came from *nguba*, a word for peanuts in the Bantu language of Africa.) Confederate soldiers sometimes had nothing to eat but goober peas, or were forced to use them, ground and boiled, as a substitute for coffee. Eating peanuts inspired some anonymous Confederate soldier to write an ironic song about the experience.

> *Sitting by the roadside, on a summer day,*
> *Chatting with my messmates, passing time away,*
> *Lying in the shadows, underneath the trees,*
> *Goodness how delicious, eating goober peas!*
> *Peas! Peas! Peas! Peas! Eating goober peas!*
> *Goodness how delicious, eating goober peas!*[5]

Union soldiers fighting in the South also found themselves eating goober peas and sometimes even enjoying them. After the war was over in 1865, they carried the memory back home with them. Soon white people all over the United States were taking a new look at peanuts.

DUMPING ROASTED PEANUTS IN PAN.

STEAM PEANUT WAGON.

Street vendors selling roasted peanuts began to appear in large cities, many of them former soldiers who could find no other jobs. Around 1870, Phineas T. Barnum decided that peanuts would make a great snack for the crowds attending his circuses. Peanuts were also sold at ball games and even at theater performances. The inexpensive balcony seats in theaters came to be known as "peanut galleries" because their occupants ate such large quantities of this cheap snack.

Roasted and salted peanuts were well established as a snack food in the United States by the late 1800s, when another important step in the peanut's new career was taken. A doctor in St. Louis,

A street vendor selling peanuts in New York City during the 1890s.

Missouri, created peanut butter as a nutritious, easily eaten food for elderly patients. Made of finely ground roasted peanuts (sometimes with the addition of sugar and salt), peanut butter was similar to the thick peanut sauces used by cooks in other parts of the world. In the United States, peanut butter spread on bread, sometimes with jelly or jam, became popular mainly as a food for young people. Today about one-half of all peanuts grown in the United States are made into peanut butter.

61

In his laboratory at the Tuskegee Institute, George Washington Carver developed all kinds of products that could be made out of peanuts.

George Washington Carver, a black scientist who was born a slave, tried to show Americans that the peanut was good for more than just peanut butter. Working at Tuskegee Institute in Alabama from 1903 until his death in 1943, Carver developed over three hundred products that could be made from the leaves, shells, and nuts of the peanut plant. His peanut products included such inedible items as soaps, dyes, and shaving cream, but he also made cheese, coffee, ice cream, and mayonnaise out of peanuts. Carver's research also led to improvements in peanut production and harvesting.

Despite George Washington Carver's inventive research, most North Americans continued to think of peanuts mainly as crunchy snacks or as the raw material of peanut butter. But today the peanut's reputation may be changing. Many African Americans are rediscovering the cooking traditions of their ancestors, which often include spicy groundnut stew. Some American cities now have restaurants specializing in food from Thailand or Indonesia. Here satay is served along with the traditional peanut sauce made with hot peppers and coconut milk. If you try one of these peanut dishes from other parts of the world, you may never look at peanut butter in the same way again.

POTATOES
Buried Treasure

Europeans first encountered most of the New World's food plants in the Caribbean islands and Mexico. Almost as soon as Christopher Columbus and his crew disembarked from their ships in 1492, they found maize and *aji* (peppers) growing on the island of Hispaniola.

Soon after Hernán Cortés reached Mexico in 1519, he was eating maize tortillas seasoned with *chillies* (again, peppers) and sipping the Aztec cacao drink, *cacaoatl*. When the invading Spaniards toured the great outdoor market in Tenochtitlán, the Aztec capital, they saw not only maize, *chillies*, and cacao seeds but also dozens of varieties of tomatoes and beans.

But one very important American plant food was not for sale in the Aztec marketplace. It was unknown to the Aztecs and the Maya, as well as to the people of North America and the tropical Caribbean islands. This plant, the potato, could be found only in South America, growing high on the slopes of the Andes Mountains.

These lofty mountains and the regions surrounding them had been home to Native American civilizations for thousands of years. As early as 1000 B.C., people were building cities and growing crops near the coast of present-day Peru and on the high plateaus between the mountain ranges of the Andes.

More than two thousand years later, the whole Andes region was controlled by the powerful Inca Empire. This "great kingdom," according to the Spanish priest Bernabe Cobo, "extended from north to south . . . for a distance of nine hundred to one thousand . . . leagues [2,500 miles]" and had its capital in the "royal city of Cuzco, like the heart in the middle of the body."[1]

Newcomers like the Aztecs in Mexico, the Incas had seized power in Peru around A.D. 1400. Their empire was to last for an even shorter time than that of the Aztecs. In 1532, the Spaniard Francisco Pizarro, leading a troop of about 260 men, invaded Peru in search of gold. After Pizarro kidnapped and killed the emperor Atahuallpa, the Inca Empire crumbled. (It had been weakened by European diseases that had spread from Mexico.)

Pizarro and his followers did find gold in Peru. The walls of Inca temples were covered with whole sheets of the precious metal. Europeans melted down what they could get their hands on and shipped it home to Spain. But in their greed for gold, they almost overlooked an even greater treasure buried in the soil.

Potatoes had been grown in Peru for centuries before the Incas ruled the land. Domesticated as early as 3000 B.C., potatoes thrived in the mountain climate of the Andes region, despite cool days and long, frosty nights. Native farmers raised crops of potatoes on terraces

A Moche stirrup jar in the shape of a potato with a human head. The Moche people often showed plants and animals with human features in their pottery, perhaps for religious reasons.

These drawings by Incan artist Guaman Poma de Ayala show potatoes being planted (top) and harvested (bottom) with the use of a *taclla*, or foot plow.

carved out of mountain slopes and irrigated by water brought from distant rivers.[2] They developed many varieties that differed in color, size, taste, and growing requirements. Peruvian potatoes might have skins that were brown, red, orange, pink, purple, or almost black. Some were no bigger than walnuts, while others were the size of grapefruits.

By the time the Incas came on the scene in the early 1400s, the people of Peru were eating some other basic foods along with potatoes. One was maize, the plant that was king in most of the Americas. Among the Incas, particularly the rich and powerful, the maize beer *chicha* was very popular. Bernabe Cobo claimed that many Peruvians were addicted to this intoxicating beverage.[3] To insure an adequate supply of the drink, the Inca emperor sometimes forced his subjects to move from their homes in the mountains to lower areas so that they could raise maize for the royal storage bins. (Maize will not grow above eleven thousand feet in altitude, whereas potatoes thrive at up to fifteen thousand feet.)

Despite the popularity of *chicha* and other forms of maize, most ordinary Incas continued to depend on potatoes. Known as *papas* in Quechua, the Inca language, potatoes were eaten every day, along with beans, peppers, and a variety of other plant foods. They were often made into stews or soups along with another Peruvian staple, *quinoa*, a grain from a plant in the pigweed family. These dishes might also include meat from *cuys*, or guinea pigs, which ordinary Inca people raised inside their houses. (Modern Peruvians do the same.)

Cooks in ancient Peru could use either fresh potatoes or *chuno* in their dishes. *Chuno*, which Father Cobo described as the Peruvians' "substitute for bread,"[4] was made of potatoes processed in a special way. Fresh potatoes were first spread on the ground and left there overnight, where they froze in the cold mountain air. The following day, after the potatoes had thawed, people trampled on them, forcing out the water they contained. This process was

A woman brings a cup of the maize beer *chicha* to workers planting potatoes.

repeated several times until the potatoes became very dry and light, almost like pieces of plastic foam. In this "freeze-dried" form, they would keep almost indefinitely.

Fresh or dried, potatoes were an essential part of Inca life. To Europeans, however, they were a new and very strange food. The Spaniards who invaded Peru in the 1530s tried potatoes and found them good to eat ("a dainty dish even for Spaniards,"[5] said one taster). But they were puzzled about just what kind of food these *papas* were.

Many early Spanish accounts associated potatoes with truffles. One conquistador remarked that "these papas are a kind of truffle, which one uses instead of bread."[6] Even Francisco Pizarro was reported to say that the potato was like "a mealy, tasty truffle."[7] Today most people in the United States probably think of a truffle as an expensive kind of chocolate candy, but the word orginally referred to an edible fungus (this is still its primary meaning). What connection could potatoes possibly have with a fungus? The link, as least in the eyes of Europeans in the 1500s, was that both were found

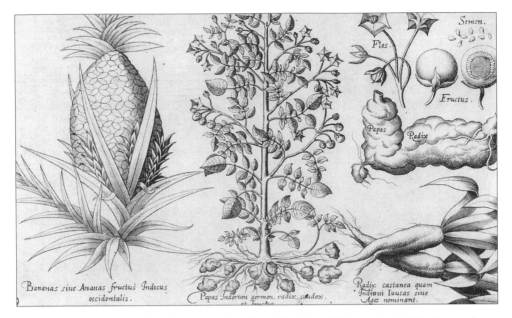

Bananas siue Ananas fructus Indicus occidentalis.

Papas Indorum germen, radix, caudex, et fructus.

Radix castanea quam Indiani Iuucas siue Ages nominant.

This drawing from a book about the New World published in 1621 shows the potato plant (center), along with its flower, fruit, and tuber (upper right). Two other American plants, the pineapple (left) and the sweet potato (lower right), are also pictured.

underground. Truffles form under the soil at the foot of oak or beech trees. Potatoes are also buried in the earth. They are tubers, underground sections of the potato plant stem that serve as storage places for nutrients.

Europeans in the 1500s did not know much about tuber-producing plants. They were familiar with plants such as carrots and turnips, whose roots could be eaten, but the potato didn't seem to have much in common with these. The potato was also puzzling because of the way it was grown. Most of the plants that Europeans knew developed from seeds sown in the ground. But in South America, the Spaniards had observed that people planted sections of the potatoes themselves, which then grew into new potato plants. (The "eyes" of potatoes contain tiny buds that will sprout under the proper conditions.)

When Spaniards brought the potato to Europe sometime in the late 1500s, the confusion about the American plant continued. Potatoes arrived in

Spain around 1576 and in Italy during the 1580s. They had probably appeared in England by 1586, and in 1597 they were first mentioned in a European book. The book was the famous early herbal written by John Gerard, and he got the potato off to a very bad start in the Old World. Gerard seemed to think that the plant had come to Europe not from Peru, but from Virginia.

John Gerard was so fascinated by the American potato that he was pictured holding potato flowers in the portrait included in his herbal.

ARACHIDNA THEOPH. forte; Papas Peruánorum.

CAP. LII.
Arachid. Theoph. forte, Papas, radix.

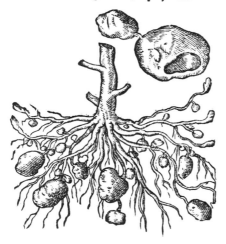

Gerard's description, entitled "Of Potatoes of Virginia," explained that the potato "grows naturally in America, where it was first discovered" and that the author had "received roots thereof from Virginia, . . . which grow and prosper in my garden as in their own native countrie."[8] This confused account convinced many people that the potato was native to Virginia, England's settlement in North America, rather than Peru, the land of the Incas.

Why did Gerard think that the Peruvian potato came from Virginia? Many historians have speculated about the reason for his mistake. Some believe it happened because the potatoes that Gerard received had actually passed through Virginia on their way from South America. According to this theory, they were probably carried by Sir Francis Drake, who stopped in Virginia in 1586 to pick up some colonists on their way home to England. Drake may have had

These drawings of potatoes from Charles L'Ecluse's herbal of 1601 are labeled "Papas Peruanorum." The French scientist knew the potato's true origins and even its correct native name.

with him potatoes that he had obtained earlier in South America. When the tubers reached Gerard in England, he became confused about their origin.

Whatever the explanation, Gerard's mistake had a long-lasting effect. For years, many people believed that potatoes came from Virginia, despite the fact that later herbals (for example, one written by the well-respected French writer Charles L'Ecluse in 1601) gave the potato's correct origins.

John Gerard insisted that the "potato of Virginia" be called by "the name proper to it"[9] because there was already a New World "potato" in England at that time. Gerard refers to this mysterious plant as the "common potato"; today we call it the sweet potato. The early history of the two American "potatoes" in Europe is very complicated but also very revealing. Here is a simplified account of what happened.

In the 1500s, sweet potatoes were growing on the islands of the Caribbean and in other warm parts of the Americas, including the lowland regions of Peru. The thickened roots of the plants were a common food item in these areas. In the Taino language spoken by many Caribbean people, they were called *batatas*.

Europeans learned about *batatas* early in their travels in the New World, and they were very impressed by their rich, sweet taste. One Spaniard who tried them in the Caribbean said that they tasted just like "fine marzipan" (a sweet made from almond paste and sugar). Another claimed that roasted *batatas* were so honey-sweet that they seemed to have been dipped in a jar of jam.[10]

Batatas probably arrived in Spain soon after 1492, where they became known as *patatas*. English-speaking people picked up this name and changed it even further to become *potatoes*. But things really got complicated when the "*papas*" from Peru (modern white potatoes) showed up in Europe in the late 1500s. Europeans assumed that these new plants were related to the well-known and very popular *batatas* (modern sweet potatoes). So they called them by the same name, creating great confusion for later researchers. (Actually, the plants have no botanical relationship.)

Eventually, Europeans began to distinguish between the two American imports. At first, English people followed John Gerard's misleading suggestion and referred to the potato from Peru as the "potato from Virginia." As the plant's popularity grew, however, it gradually became *the* potato or sometimes the white potato. (Later in its history, it would be known as the Irish potato.) The "other" potatoes—the Caribbean *batatas*—became sweet potatoes, and this is where things stand today in most English-speaking countries.

When *the* potato first arrived in Europe, it did not get the same kind of warm reception as its supposed relative, the sweet potato. Although Spanish explorers and settlers in Peru had eaten potatoes and enjoyed them, the people back home did not find them so appealing. They were put off by the fact that the potato was an underground tuber, and they also found its lumpy shape unappetizing. (Early varieties were much lumpier than the smooth, oval potatoes we know today.)

Even worse, Europeans suspected that potatoes might cause disease. This accusation was also made against the tomato and other food plants from the Americas that had little in common with familiar European plants. (American beans were never thought to be dangerous.) But the potato was considered a special threat because it was linked with one of the most dreaded diseases known in Europe, leprosy. This connection was made largely because of the potato's rough and lumpy skin, which reminded Europeans of the terrible skin sores and growths caused by leprosy.

Potatoes were so feared as a source of disease in some parts of Europe that laws were passed against eating them. This apparently happened in Burgundy (a region now part of France) during the early 1600s. According to Gaspard Bauhin, the author of an herbal published in 1620, "Burgundians are forbidden to make use of these tubers because they are assured that the eating of them causes leprosy."[11]

Some Europeans considered potatoes dangerous for very different rea-

Serpillum citratum.   Papas Peruanorum.   *Thymus vulgaris.*

The lumpy potato tuber shown in this picture suggests why Europeans often associated the plant with the skin growths caused by leprosy. From a German herbal of 1613, this drawing also includes two varieties of the herb thyme.

Batatas.

Camotes.
Amotes.
Ajcs.

Vſus.

The potato got its reputation as an aphrodisiac because of its association with the *batata*, or sweet potato.

sons. Like tomatoes, they were thought to be an aphrodisiac, a food that aroused human passions. This reputation came mainly because of their association with sweet potatoes. Almost as soon as the sweet, rich-tasting *batata* arrived in Europe, it was reported to inspire lust, or as many writers of the day delicately put it, "incite to Venus." Because the humble white potato was considered a close relative of the sweet potato, it was thought to have the same power. Later, when populations began to grow in Ireland and other potato-eating countries, people were sure that it was due to the potato's lusty influence.

These strange beliefs lasted a long time, but eventually Europeans discovered other more practical qualities in the American potato. One was the ease with which it could be cultivated. Unlike many other New World foods, which required warmth to grow, potatoes flourished in the cool climate of northern Europe.

Although countries such as England, Scotland, Ireland, Germany, and Russia couldn't grow American maize or peanuts, they had perfect conditions for growing potatoes.

Potatoes also proved to be a very productive crop. Growing them did not require a lot of land or a great deal of time and labor. Three months after a potato crop was planted, it was ready for harvest. Even better, land planted in potatoes yielded five times the amount of food as wheat or even maize. The quantity was not only greater, but more nourishment was also provided for human use. Although potatoes are 80 percent water, they contain significant amounts of carbohydrates as well as several vitamins, particularly vitamin C. (The potato's "biological value," measured in the amount of nitrogen supplied to the human body, is 73, compared to 72 for soybeans, 54 for maize, and 53 for wheat.)

One final advantage that the potato had over wheat and other grains was, ironically, one of the things that Europeans had first disliked about the American plant. The part of the potato plant that people ate was the tuber, which grew underground. Here it was safe from wind, hail, and other kinds of severe weather that could destroy a grain crop, which had its edible parts above ground.

Despite all the potato's good qualities, European farmers in the 1600s and 1700s did not rush to plant them. Potatoes were considered "insipid and starchy," a food "for those who only look to it to maintain themselves."[12] It took many long years, and some drastic efforts, before large numbers of Europeans were converted to growing the American tubers.

In some countries, governments even got involved in convincing their citizens that potatoes were worth eating. This is what happened in Prussia (part of present-day Germany). During the late 1600s, the country was hit by several crop failures that caused widespread famine. The Prussian ruler, Frederick William, decided that his subjects would be better off if they grew potatoes. So he issued an order that all peasants had to plant potatoes or risk having their noses and ears cut off. This convincing argument persuaded many to try the American tubers, and it wasn't long before ordinary Prussians decided that they were a valuable crop.

Potatoes became so popular in Prussia that they even played a part in a war fought in the late 1700s. In 1778, Frederick the Great of Prussia engaged in a struggle with neighboring Austria during which the opposing armies destroyed the potato crops in their enemy's fields. Because of this tactic, the conflict became popularly known as the *Kartoffelkrieg*, or Potato War. (Its formal name was the War of Bavarian Succession.)

Another war was indirectly responsible for getting the people of France to try potatoes. During the Seven Years War, which lasted from 1756 to 1763, Antoine Parmentier, a pharmacist serving in the French army, was captured and imprisoned in Prussia for three long years. Fed a diet of potatoes while in prison, Parmentier returned to France convinced that the American tubers would make an ideal crop for French farmers. In 1771, he wrote a prize-winning academic paper recommending the potato as a nourishing vegetable "that in times of necessity could be substituted for ordinary food."

Parmentier's potato campaign took a big step forward when it got the attention of royalty. In 1785, Parmentier impressed King Louis XVI and Queen Marie Antoinette by presenting them with a basket full of potatoes and a bouquet of potato flowers. (The queen put some flowers in her hair, starting a fad among women of the French nobility.) In a more practical vein, Parmentier demonstrated the potato's versatility by serving the king, queen, and royal court a meal of twenty different potato dishes.

To convince commoners of the tuber's appeal, Parmentier used another clever tactic. He planted potatoes in a field on the outskirts of Paris and stationed soldiers to guard it during the day. At night, the soldiers left, allowing curious people the opportunity to investigate the field and perhaps to take a sample of the precious crop.

Antoine Parmentier displays his first crop of potatoes to King Louis XVI of France.

Parmentier's efforts on behalf of the potato were effective. During the late 1700s, French farmers discovered the advantages of growing potatoes, and French cooks learned to make appetizing dishes out of them. Potato soup made with rich cream and butter became popular, and one version was even named Potage Parmentier in honor of the potato's great champion. In a later period, French cooks would present the world with the ultimate form of potatoes, french fries—which really did originate in France.

During the 1700s, many countries in northern Europe turned to potatoes as a staple crop. In Russia, Empress Catherine the Great encouraged her subjects to plant potatoes in 1765 after severe famines had devastated the country. Poland, Holland, Belgium, and the Scandinavian countries all discovered that potatoes could provide a nourishing and reliable diet for people without much land or other resouces.

In some parts of Europe, this new food plant, along with other foods from the Americas, helped make possible some important social and political changes. With more food available, fewer people died in famines or were killed by diseases caused by malnutrition. As a result, populations began to rise. Countries that were once weak and unable to defend themselves now became more powerful and capable of playing a bigger role on the world stage. The European world was changing, and the American potato was part of that change.[13]

Of all the countries of northern Europe, Ireland was the one in which potatoes became most important. And it was in Ireland that the American tubers became part of a terrible human tragedy.

The potato had reached Ireland very early in its European travels. No one knows exactly how it arrived there, but there are several intriguing stories about the event. Some accounts credit Sir Walter Raleigh, the dashing English explorer and soldier, with bringing potatoes to Ireland from the Americas in the late 1500s. Others give Sir Francis Drake the honor of having introduced the potato to England and Ireland.

Still others claim that in 1588, the Irish took potatoes from the holds of Spanish ships that had been wrecked off the coast of Ireland. These ships were part of the great fleet known as the Armada, which had been sent by Spain to invade England but was defeated by the English navy. (Ships from the Armada were destroyed by storms on the Irish coast, but whether they contained potatoes, no one really knows.)

However and whenever they arrived in Ireland, potatoes had become well established there by the mid-1600s. The cool, moist Irish climate was ideal for growing the American plant. Other conditions existing in Ireland also made the potato very welcome there. For many years, the country had been torn by warfare and by conflict with the controlling power of England. During the 1600s and 1700s, large sections of land in Ireland were owned by landlords who lived in England but who often used their Irish estates to produce crops or animals for export. Most Irish people had little or no land of their own and few resources. They lived in poverty and were frequent victims of famine and disease.

When the potato arrived from the Americas, it made a tremendous difference in the lives of ordinary Irish people. They could grow potatoes on small plots of rented land, without the use of expensive tools or animals for plowing. A little more than one acre could supply enough potatoes to feed a family of five for a year. The crop stayed safely underground until time for harvest, hidden from the armies that continually marched across Irish soil.

By the end of the 1700s, the average person in Ireland ate eight to ten pounds of potatoes each day. And he or she ate very little else. The diet consisted of boiled potatoes, sometimes accompanied by cabbage, turnips, and milk. An old saying summed up the course of a typical Irish meal: "While you're eating your first potato, peel the second, don't put down the third, and keep your eye on the fourth."[14] Even the family cow was fed on potatoes boiled in the same pot used for human meals.

With this steady supply of monotonous but nourishing food, the population began to grow in Ireland, just as it had in other countries after the potato made its appearance. In the period from 1754 to 1845, the population increased from 3.2 million people to almost 8.2 million. And all these millions depended on potatoes for their daily food. They did not know how to grow anything else and had no other source of nourishment.

In 1845, disaster struck the "Irish" potato and the people of Ireland. All over the country, potato plants turned black in the fields almost overnight and then died. When the potatoes were dug up, most were rotten. Some of the Irish crop escaped destruction that year, but in 1846, the potatoes were again attacked by the terrible plant disease, which was a kind of fungus. "This year, scarcely a plant in the whole four provinces [of Ireland] was spared—

A drawing from an 1849 newspaper shows an Irish woman searching for potatoes in a field.

the destruction of the crop was all but complete; the terror and desolation it brought in its train, no less."[15]

The following year saw some relief, but in 1848 and 1849, the disease again raged, despite desperate efforts to eradicate it. The Irish people, whose lives had depended on potatoes for more than two hundred years, were left with nothing to eat.

Soon thousands were dying of starvation and diseases that attacked bodies weakened by hunger. The rest of the world made some effort to help by sending food supplies. (The British government sent American maize to Ireland, but no one knew what to do with this strange foreign grain.) These measures, however, were too small to have any effect.

By the time that the Irish Potato Famine had run its course in 1849, a million and a half people were dead. About the same number had fled Ireland in search of better lives in other lands.

Many of these immigrants made their way to the United States. During the 1850s, a million Irish men, women, and children boarded ships that were headed for the American land of opportunity. Despite poverty and discrimination, they did make better lives in the new land. The Irish found their beloved potatoes growing in the northeastern United States (they had come over with immigrants from Ireland in the 1700s), and they continued to be

Fleeing the Potato Famine in Ireland, immigrants wait for ships that will take them to Boston, New York, and other cities in North America.

potato eaters. Soon other Americans were calling the tubers "spuds," an Irish nickname derived from *spade*, the garden tool used wherever potatoes were grown.

By the 1800 and 1900s, potatoes had found their way to many parts of the world with climates suitable for their cultivation. They had taken root in the northern part of India, in China, and even in some of the cooler regions of Africa. Countries too warm for the "white" potato could—and did—grow sweet potatoes. This New World plant provided food for humans and animals in many parts of Asia, including Indonesia, Japan, and particularly China. Today China is the world's largest producer of sweet potatoes, and millions of Chinese people depend on the American *batatas* for their daily food.

Russia leads the world in the production of the "other" potato with the many names. China, Poland, and the United States are also major producers. As far as consumption of potatoes goes, Germans probably top the list. A

Harvesting potatoes in modern Pakistan. Today both the white potato and the sweet potato are grown in many areas around the world.

study done in the 1980s showed that each person living in East Germany ate about 370 pounds of potatoes every year. Today there is only one Germany, and its citizens are still cooking and eating a lot of potatoes.

Simple and basic, the potato can be cooked in a great variety of ways, and German cooks have come up with some delicious potato recipes. They combine boiled potatoes with apples and bacon to make a hearty and appetizing dish called *Himmel und Erde* (Heaven and Earth). Germans make pancakes out of grated raw potatoes, which they fry golden brown in butter and eat with sweet applesauce. (Jewish cooks in Europe and the United States make similar potato pancakes called *latkes*.) Potato dumplings and hot potato salad with bacon and vinegar are other potato dishes often found on German tables.

Once cooks in France decided that potatoes were worth eating, they used their culinary skills to transform the humble potato. They made savory soups like Potage Parmentier, which often combined potatoes with leeks, a delicately flavored member of the onion family. They also prepared scalloped and au gratin potatoes by baking sliced potatoes combined with cheese, butter, cream, and bread crumbs.

French cooks have been "french frying" slices of potatoes in hot oil since the late 1700s. When Thomas Jefferson served as the American ambassador to France in 1789, he learned to like french fries. In fact, he liked them so much that when he became president of the United States a few years later, he had the White House chef prepare them for his dinner guests. The French liked fried potatoes so much that they came up with a way of frying them *twice*, creating golden, puffy soufflé potatoes.

Today people all over the world eat french-fried potatoes, dipping them in ketchup, mayonnaise, vinegar, and many other kinds of sauces. Also enjoyed around the world are potato chips, a U.S. contribution to potato cookery. These thin, crisp-fried potato slices were invented by accident in the 1870s. The original chips started out as french fries on the menu at a resort in Saratoga Springs, New York. Diners at the resort restaurant were complaining that the slices of fried potatoes were too thick, so the chef cut some potatoes as thin as paper and fried them in hot oil. His customers thought they were terrific, and the "Saratoga" chip was born. In the United States, the name was later changed to potato chip. In England, however, potato chips meant french-fried potatoes, so the new chips became potato "crisps."

As crisps, chips, and fries, potatoes have become the ultimate snack food. But they are also a basic ingredient in cooking around the world, used in dishes that are filling, nourishing, and satisfying. Although most people don't depend on potatoes for their daily food as the Irish did in the 1700s and 1800s, potatoes are on the international dinner table frequently and in many delicious disguises.

TOMATOES
Forbidden Fruit

In the modern world of cooking and eating, the tomato is everywhere. Supermarket shelves are stocked with cans of whole tomatoes and stewed tomatoes, with tomato juice, paste, puree, and sauce. In fast-food restaurants from New York to Tokyo, people put spicy-sweet tomato ketchup on their hamburgers and french fries. Pasta and pizza usually come topped with savory sauces made from tomatoes. And the plump red tomato—glossy, juicy, and brimming with flavor—is the most highly prized vegetable grown in backyard gardens.

Today tomatoes are eaten and enjoyed just about everywhere. But it was not so long ago that they were considered an exotic food in many places and even viewed with suspicion and distrust. Up until the mid-1800s, many Europeans and North Americans thought that tomatoes were poisonous. Others might have been willing to eat them but were not sure how. Tomatoes were brightly colored and juicy, like peaches and other fruits, but their taste was acidic and rather salty. Were they fruits or vegetables? Should they be eaten fresh or cooked? Just what kind of food were they?

TOMATOES

Before the early 1500s, no one in Europe, Asia, or Africa had ever seen or heard of this strange food plant. Like maize, potatoes, and peppers, tomatoes were cultivated and eaten only in the Americas. Unlike these very important foods, however, tomatoes were not widely grown in the New World. The people of ancient Mexico, particularly the Aztecs, deserve the credit for giving tomatoes to the world.

Wild plants in the tomato family are found today in many parts of western South America near the Andes mountain range. But the ancient people of this region apparently did not grow tomatoes as a cultivated plant. It was in Mexico that tomatoes were domesticated, perhaps from wild plants that grew from seeds brought from South America by birds.

When Cortés and his followers invaded the Aztec Empire in 1519, they became the first non-Americans to see tomatoes. Either they weren't very impressed by this food plant, or it was not in very common use. Only a few Spanish accounts mention tomatoes as an item in the Aztec diet.

As usual, Friar Bernardino de Sahagún provides the most information. According to his observations, the Aztecs used tomatoes in cooked sauces that also contained capsicum peppers. Sahagún describes tomato sauces with red, green, hot, and yellow *chillies* that were sold in the cooked-food section of the great marketplace at Tenochtitlán, the Aztec capital.[1]

The observant Spanish friar also tells us that tomatoes were among the fresh foods offered at the market. Sahagún lists many varieties available to Aztec cooks: "large tomatoes, small tomatoes, leaf tomatoes, thin tomatoes, sweet tomatoes, . . . those which are yellow, very yellow, quite yellow, red, very red, . . . bright red, reddish, rosy dawn colored."[2]

Friar Sahagún's list tells us one very important thing: There was not just one "tomato" in the Aztec world. The English word *tomato* comes from the Spanish *tomate*, which was taken directly from a Nahuatl word, *tomatl*. But the Aztecs grew several plants with this same root name. One of these was the *xitomatl*, the familiar red tomato known around the world today. Other

Poma amoris fructu
rubro.

As this drawing from an herbal published in 1613 shows, early tomatoes in
Europe had more lobes and grooves than the smooth modern tomatoes.

varieties were the *coyotomatl* and the *coaxitomatl*. Yet another food plant in the *tomatl* group was the *miltomatl*. Today this is usually called the husk tomato, or tomatillo. With a small green fruit enclosed in a papery husk, it belongs to a completely different scientific family than the popular red tomato.[3]

Most early Spanish accounts shortened all the Nahuatl words ending in -*tomatl* to one Spanish word, *tomate*. Because of this change, no one is really sure what kind of "tomatoes" were used in Aztec sauces. In parts of Mexico today, the tomatillo is more common in cooked dishes than the red tomato, and this may have been true in ancient times as well. But the *tomatl* that traveled around the world was definitely not the tomatillo.

Conquistadores probably brought seeds of the *xitomatl* and a few other varieties back to Spain in the early 1500s. The plants did not make a big splash in the European world. In 1554, they began appearing in a few herbals, but no one seemed to know much about their use or origins. An Italian writer, Pietro Matthioli, mentioned the tomato in connection with the eggplant, another exotic edible. He noted the two plants' similarities (in fact, they belong to the same scientific family). Matthioli also said that tomatoes "were cooked in the same way as eggplants: fried in oil with salt and pepper."[4]

By the end of the 1500s, the tomato had become more widely known but not much more popular in most parts of Europe. In 1597, the English herbalist John Gerard claimed that the whole plant had a "ranke and stinking savour" (he was probably referring to the strong smell of the leaves). He said that tomatoes grew "in Spain, Italy and such hot Countries," where they were eaten "boiled with pepper, salt and oyle; but they yeeld very little nourishment to the body."[5]

In describing this unattractive and not very nourishing plant, Gerard did not use the word *tomato* or any other word that might have come from the original Nahuatl name. Instead he referred to it as the "Apple of Love" and the "Golden Apple." The story behind these seemingly inappropriate English

This illustration from John Gerard's herbal pictures the "love apples" so feared and despised by people in northern Europe.

names is part of the strange history of the tomato in Europe.

The names Apple of Love and Golden Apple come from early words for the American *tomatl* that were used in Italy and several other European countries. Italy and Spain were the first places in Europe where the tomato was accepted as a food. During the 1600s, cooks in both of these Mediterranean countries prepared tomatoes in sauces very similar to the ones made by the Aztecs. American peppers, both the hot and the sweet varieties, were also ingredients in early tomato recipes from Spain and Italy.[6]

In Spain, *tomate* was the word used for this American food plant, but in Italy, it was known as *pomo d'oro* (golden apple). In France, the tomato had yet another name—*pomme d'amour* (apple of love). Where did these odd names come from? The "apple" part is not too difficult to understand. Apples were ancient and very familiar food plants in Europe. Since tomatoes did resemble apples somewhat in shape and also in color, it is not surprising that these exotic imports from the Americas were given that name.

Tomatoes may have been called "golden apples" because the ones that first appeared in some parts of Europe were probably yellow rather than red. Friar

Sahagún tells us that the Aztecs had yellow *tomatls*, and these varieties may have been among those transported to the Old World.

Other explanations for these strange names have more to do with history than botany. One idea is that they may have come from the name for another glossy, smooth-skinned food, the eggplant. In Italy during the 1600s, the eggplant was known as *pomo di mori*, apple of the Moors. The French called it by a similar name, *pomme des mours*. These names originated because the eggplant had come to Europe from North Africa, where it was a popular ingredient in the cooking of Moorish people.

Many Europeans considered the eggplant as distasteful and dangerous as the American tomato. And the two exotic plants were closely related, both of them members of the scientific family Solanaceae. Because of these connections, some historians believe that the names *pomo d'oro* and *pomme d'amour* are actually mispronounced versions of "apple of the Moors," which somehow became attached to the tomato early in its travels in Europe.[7]

Whatever the explanation for their origins, these names continued to be used in Europe for many hundreds of years. In France, the tomato was known as *pomme d'amour* up until the 1800s. *Pomodoro* is the name used in Italy yet today. For English-speaking people, "love apple" became a common name for the tomato, bringing with it all kinds of disturbing associations.

For centuries, many people in England and in other northern European countries believed that the tomato, like the potato, was an aphrodisiac. They were sure that eating "love apples" aroused passionate feelings in humans. The resemblance of the plump red tomato to the popular image of the human heart may have had something to do with this belief. Whatever the reason, upright and moral people would not have anything to do with this dangerous food. At most, they would grow the tomato as an ornamental plant, cautiously admiring its yellow flowers and bright red fruits.

Tomatoes were also suspect in northern European countries because they were believed to be poisonous. As Europeans were well aware, the tomato was related not only to the eggplant but also to deadly nightshade, a poisonous member of the family Solanaceae. If tomatoes were not actually poisonous, then eating them would certainly cause disease. These fears, added to the tomato's generally unsavory reputation, made it a food to be avoided.

While northern Europeans were giving tomatoes the cold shoulder, people in Spain, Italy, and other Mediterranean countries were quietly making them an important part of their cuisines. The sunny climate in these southern regions was ideal for growing tomatoes. In many areas, every house had a small garden or a pot on the windowsill in which tomato plants flourished.

Spain found many uses for the tomato, incorporating it into traditional dishes that had existed for centuries. One of these dishes was gazpacho, originally an uncooked soup made out of stale bread, oil, water, vinegar, and garlic. When fresh tomatoes were added to this mixture, as well as cucumbers and sweet peppers, gazpacho began to change from a soup into a kind of liquid salad. The original soupy "white" gazpacho can still be found in Spain today, but the rest of the world usually makes it with tomatoes.[8]

In Spain and Italy, just as in ancient Mexico, tomatoes were most often used in sauces. But now they were combined with typical European ingredients such as onions, garlic, and olive oil rather than hot peppers. In southern Italy, tomato sauces came to be used over spaghetti and other kinds of pasta. Italians had been eating these noodles made of wheat-flour paste since the 1400s. Toppings for pasta dishes usually consisted of olive oil, cheese, butter, or mashed cooked vegetables such as carrots. But after the introduction of the tomato in the 1500s, the popularity of tomato sauces began to grow. By the 1800s, they had become the most common pasta topping in many areas of southern Italy.

Tomatoes also became part of another southern Italian specialty, pizza.

This flat bread baked with various toppings had been made in Italy for centuries. The modern pizza, topped with cheese and tomato sauce, originated in the city of Naples in the 1600s. But its biggest success came when it was brought to the United States three hundred years later.

Crisp pizza pie covered with bubbling cheese and savory tomato sauce didn't reach the shores of North America until the early 1900s. If it had come much earlier, it would not have gotten a very good reception. Many North Americans were as suspicious of tomatoes and tomato dishes as were people from northern Europe.

Most of the early settlers in North America came from England and other northern European countries. Like the people back home, the colonists were convinced that the tomato was dangerous and ungodly. Others were put off by the tomato's unusual taste or by the strong smell of the plant's leaves.

But tomatoes were not unpopular everywhere in North America during the 1700s and 1800s. Many people in the southeastern United States knew and liked them. Tomatoes had been grown by Spaniards in Florida during colonial times, and their use had slowly spread to other regions of the South. Black slaves who came to southern plantations from the Caribbean also brought with them a love of tomatoes and the seeds to grow them. At his home in Virginia, Thomas Jefferson, always a freethinker and experimenter, raised tomatoes during the early 1800s and served them fresh at his dinner table.

According to a well-known story, it was a single important event that finally convinced most Americans to eat tomatoes. That event supposedly took place in 1820, when Colonel Robert Gibbon Johnson, a veteran of the Revolutionary War, set out to prove that tomatoes were not dangerous. On September 26, standing on the steps of the courthouse in Salem, New Jersey, Colonel Johnson ate a whole basketful of tomatoes. He suffered no immediate ill effects and did not develop high blood pressure, brain fever, or cancer.

(These were some of the diseases supposedly caused by eating tomatoes.)

Colonel Johnson really did exist, but his exploit may be only legend. Research has revealed no historical evidence that he ever actually stood on the courthouse steps and ate all those tomatoes. Yet the story has been repeated in many books and magazine articles. Since 1987, it has even been reenacted every year in Salem, with an actor dressed as Johnson devouring tomatoes in front of the courthouse.[9]

TOMATO, TURNER HYBRID.

Tomatoes.

Turner Hybrid. This grand Tomato is entirely different from all others, particularly in foliage, which is entire, and not cut. It is a rank grower and enormously productive, outyielding all others. The fruit is extra large in size and very solid. They have very few seeds and no hard core, and are unequalled in fine flavor. Without hesitation we pronounce it the most valuable of all Tomatoes. Pkt., 10c.; oz., 85c.

Cardinal. In this new Tomato are combined all the good qualities of the many sorts now before the public. Its shape is perfectly round, solid and smooth; flavor the best, and fewer seeds than any other sort. Its color is brilliant cardinal red, which, with its smoothness and fine shape, makes it most beautiful. Pkt., 10c.; oz., 60c.

Trophy. Large red. Pkt., 5c.; oz., 30c.

President Garfield. A new German variety weighing two or three pounds. Pkt., 10c.

Whether Colonel Johnson's feat is legend or fact, the tomato did eventually lose its bad reputation during the 1800s and find its way into American kitchens. Changes taking place in the United States population helped to make this possible. Immigrants from southern Italy began arriving in the late 1880s, bringing with them a tradition of cooking with tomatoes and recipes for delicious tomato dishes. In 1876, another momentous event in the tomato's history took place: H. J. Heinz put on the market the first bottle of commercially produced tomato ketchup.

Homemade sauces called ketchup or catsup had existed in the United States before Heinz's creation. They had had an even longer history in England, where they had been around since the early 1700s. Early ketchups were

Varieties of hybrid tomatoes advertised in a seed catalog from 1889.

modeled after spicy sauces that British traders had learned about in the Far East. Called *ketchap* in the Malay language and *ketsiap* in a Chinese dialect, these sauces were usually made from pickled fish. In England, cooks used oysters or walnuts, combined with vinegar, sugar, and spices, to make their version of ketchup.

These same recipes were used in the United States during the 1700s and early 1800s. But when tomatoes became popular, their acid taste and bright red color seemed to make them a perfect ingredient for ketchup. Cooks began making and bottling tomato ketchup at home to use as a sauce for meat and a topping for potatoes. When H. J. Heinz turned out the first batch of commercially produced ketchup, he made this popular tomato sauce available to people who did not want to go to the trouble of preparing it themselves. The rest is tomato history.[10]

Just as the tomato finally made itself at home in North America, it was also accepted in European countries where it was once considered unfit to eat. Even in England, the dreaded "love apple" was acknowledged to be

Heinz ketchup bottles have gone through a lot of changes since the popular tomato sauce was first introduced in 1876.

93

A woman selling tomatoes at a market in Dakar, the capital of Senegal.

edible, at least when used fresh in sandwiches and salads. Eventually, cooks all over the world came to recognize the tomato's appeal.

In many parts of Africa today, tomatoes are now a familiar ingredient in spicy stews and vegetable dishes. Indian cooks use tomatoes in curries and chutneys. And the American *tomatl* has become one of the most common vegetables grown in China. (All the world thinks of the tomato as a vegetable even though in botanical terms, it is actually a fruit.)

Today growers can choose among more than five hundred varieties of tomatoes that have been developed to suit different climates and different uses. Popular with home gardeners are varieties with such appealing names as Early Girl, Big Boy, Beefsteak, and Brandywine. In the United States alone, commercial growers produce around nine million tons of tomatoes each year, most destined to be turned into tomato products such as ketchup, sauce, paste, and juice.

The *tomatl* has traveled a long road since Europeans first saw it growing in the gardens of the Aztecs more than four hundred years ago. Although it has not become a food important to the world economy, as maize and potatoes have, the tomato has had a significant (and delicious) effect on the way people cook and eat.

CHOCOLATE
Food of the Gods

During his visit to Central America in the mid-1500s, the Italian Girolamo Benzoni heard about a beverage that seemed to be highly regarded by the local inhabitants. "When I passed through a tribe," he reported, "if an Indian wished . . . to give me some, he would be very much surprised to see me refuse it." Benzoni was in the Americas for more than a year before he finally sampled the beverage: "Unwilling to drink nothing but water, I did as others did. The flavor is somewhat bitter, but it satisfies and refreshes the body without intoxicating."[1]

This bitter drink—esteemed by the native people "above everything"[2]—was made from chocolate. A precious commodity in the New World, chocolate became almost equally valued and cherished in the Old World. But the chocolate known to the people of the Americas was very different from the sweet treat that Europeans would come to know and love.

Chocolate in all its forms comes from an exotic tree originally found only in the Americas. This tree, the *cacao*, produces large pods that grow attached directly to the trunk and the largest branches. Within the pods are the cacao seeds (sometimes called beans), the raw material from which chocolate products are made. Cacao seeds require complicated processing before they can become "chocolate." After being removed from the pods, they must be fermented, dried, roasted, and ground.

The leaves and pods of the cacao plant, in a drawing from 1681. The Maya and Aztecs believed that cacao was a gift of the god Quetzalcoatl, the patron of agriculture. Modern scientists call the plant *Theobroma cacao*—"food of the gods, cacao."

The process of turning the seeds of the cacao into something edible was first discovered by the people of the ancient Americas. Wild cacao is native to tropical South America as well as to the hot, humid parts of Mexico and Central America. The tree was not cultivated in South America, but the inhabitants of these other regions learned thousands of years ago how to grow and process this unique crop.

One of the earliest civilizations of the Americas, the Olmecs, may have been the first to grow cacao. The name of the tree probably originated with these ancient people, who lived in Mexico as early as 1000 B.C. A later civilization, the Maya, inherited the word *cacao* from the Olmecs, along with the method of processing cacao seeds. Beginning around A.D. 200, the Maya built large cities in the tropical rain forests of present-day Mexico, Guatemala, and Honduras. These regions were ideal for cultivating cacao, and the plant became an important crop for Maya farmers.

Maya cooks roasted and ground the cacao seeds, producing a thick paste that was mixed with water and other ingredients to make a strongly flavored drink. This drink was of great importance to the Maya, as it would later be to other people of the ancient Americas. They prepared it carefully and served it on special occasions, often in containers designed specially for it. Some of these beautiful pottery vessels have been found in Maya tombs, and they actually contain residues that chemical tests prove to be cacao. Others bear inscriptions that represent the word *cacao* in Maya hieroglyphs.[3]

The Aztecs, who came to power around A.D. 1300, inherited the American tradition of using cacao. Because the Aztec homeland was located in the high mountain valleys of central Mexico, an area too cool for the tropical cacao tree, Aztec merchants had to import cacao seeds from warmer lowland areas. The Aztecs also received the seeds as tribute from people they had conquered. Tribute lists show that every year 980 loads of cacao were sent to the capital city, Tenochtitlán, each load containing 24,000 carefully counted-out seeds.

Cacao seeds were so important to the Aztecs that they served as a form of money, just as they had for the Maya centuries earlier. In the Aztec marketplace, cacao seeds could be used to buy items for sale. For example, a small cotton cloak was worth about one hundred seeds. Because the seeds were so valuable, they were even counterfeited. Unscrupulous people filled empty cacao-seed shells with clay or dirt and tried to pass them off as the real thing.

The most important use of cacao among the Aztecs was in making the precious drink that the Maya, and Olmecs before them, had made. When Spaniards arrived in Mexico in the early 1500s, they quickly became acquainted with this ancient beverage.

Not long after Hernán Cortés and his followers landed on Mexico's east coast in 1519, they were greeted by ambassadors of the emperor Moctezuma, who offered them food and drink as a sign of courtesy and peace. The drink was *cacaoatl* (cacao water), and the Spaniards did not find it appealing. "When the Indians saw that they dared not drink they tasted from all the gourds and the Spaniards then quenched their thirst with chocolate and realized what a refreshing drink it was."[4]

When Cortés and his men reached Tenochtitlán, they found out just how important this cacao drink was. Large quantities of the beverage were consumed daily by the Aztec emperor Moctezuma and members of his court. In his account of the Spanish invasion of Mexico, Bernal Díaz del Castillo, a soldier in Cortés's army, described a typical meal eaten by the emperor. Moctezuma was offered over thirty dishes, including roasted wild birds and "fruit of all the different kinds that the land produced." During the meal, servers brought to the emperor, "in cup-shaped vessels of pure gold, a certain drink made from cacao." After Moctezuma was finished, Díaz del Castillo reported, his guards and members of his household ate, consuming "over two thousand jugs of cacao, all frothed up, as they make it in Mexico."[5]

Workers making chocolate in the Aztec marketplace. (From the Florentine Codex)

"All frothed up," the Spaniards discovered, was the way that the Aztecs liked their chocolate (the Spanish word for the cacao drink). Their method of preparing it involved beating or pouring the liquid from one container to another to produce a foamy head. Bernardino de Sahagún described the way that chocolate was prepared by vendors in the Aztec marketplace. After grinding the seeds and adding water, the chocolate maker "aerates [the liquid], filters it, strains it, pours it back and forth . . . ; he makes it form a head, makes it foam."[6]

According to Sahagún, chocolate could be made with many ingredients in addition to cacao and water. Among the extras were *chillies* (hot peppers), vanilla, wild bee honey, and sweet-smelling flowers ground to a powder. Other Aztec recipes for chocolate included ground maize kernels and the seeds and leaves of various plants (in other words, herbs and spices). The drink could be served either hot or cold.

However chocolate was made, it was a drink reserved mainly for the rich and powerful. Friar Sahagún described it as "the privilege, the drink of nobles, of rulers."[7] Women, even noble ones, were usually not allowed to consume chocolate. While the men were enjoying *cacaoatl* at the end of a feast or banquet (along with a pipe of tobacco), the women drank a beverage of ground cooked maize mixed with water and seasonings.

For the Aztecs as for the Maya before them, chocolate was an important part of social and ceremonial life. Making the drink out of cacao seeds and serving it involved special rituals and customs. When chocolate first arrived in the Old World, it played a very similar role in European life.

The first cacao seeds probably reached Spain in 1528, brought by Cortés to the royal court of Charles V, the king of Spain and ruler of the Holy Roman Empire. The conquistador also brought with him instructions for processing the seeds and even the stone grinding implements used by Aztec chocolate makers. It was not long before the new drink became all the rage among the Spanish nobility.

Monks in Spanish monasteries were given the important job of preparing the cacao seeds brought from Mexico. They roasted and ground them and then formed the cacao paste into little rods or tablets. After hardening, the tablets could be wrapped and stored until needed. To make a pot of chocolate, a cook simply dissolved the tablets in water and stirred.

Spanish chocolate drinkers, like Moctezuma and his courtiers, preferred their chocolate thick and foamy. They used a special wooden stick called a *molinet* to whip the drink. For hundreds of years, European chocolate pots were made with holes in their lids through which the molinet could be inserted.

Also like the Aztecs, the Spanish added all sorts of other ingredients to the mixture of ground cacao seeds and water. Vanilla, a seasoning from the New World, was often included, but many Old World spices such as cinnamon, nutmeg, and cloves also became popular. Spaniards sometimes used hot capsicum peppers in their chocolate, as well as black pepper. They added other ingredients that might seem even stranger to modern tastes, for example, ambergris. This waxy material found in the intestines of sperm whales was used in the 1500s as a flavoring and a kind of health tonic. Chocolate with ambergris was not only tasty but also good for you.

One important change made when chocolate reached Europe was the addition of sugar. Although the Aztecs had sometimes sweetened *cacaoatl* with honey, it was usually a rather bitter drink. In Spain during the 1500s, cane sugar (which had originated in Asia) was available, although very expensive. Mixed into chocolate, the sweet white grains made the drink even more appealing. When sugarcane became an important plantation crop in the Americas during the 1600s, there was plenty of sugar for all chocolate drinkers.

Slaves on a Brazilian sugar plantation grind sugarcane in a mill powered by oxen. The white grains made from the juice of the crushed canes made chocolate a sweeter treat.

At first, Spain tried to keep other Europeans from getting their hands on the delicious and fashionable new drink. In the 1500s, cacao trees were grown only on Spanish plantations in Mexico, so Spain controlled the raw material for chocolate. But it was not long before people in Italy and France found out about the rich, foamy beverage. Cacao seeds were smuggled out of Spain and Mexico, and soon other well-to-do Europeans were roasting, grinding, and whipping chocolate, just as they did in Spain.

In France, chocolate became the drink of the upper class in the early 1600s, when a French king married a Spanish princess. The princess brought with her to her new home the chocolate-drinking habit and a supply of the precious cacao seeds. Another royal marriage between Spain and France took place in 1660 when Marie Theresa married Louis XIV, the French monarch whose nickname was the Sun King. In Louis's splendid palace at Versailles, chocolate was the beverage of choice, particularly at breakfast. Ladies of the court had chocolate served in their bedrooms and sometimes invited guests to join them for the morning treat.

In France as in other European countries, chocolate was considered a healthful and invigorating way to start the day. (Cacao does in fact contain a little caffeine as well as another mild stimulant called *theobromine*.) In 1671, a French aristocrat, the marquise de Sévigné, wrote a letter to her daughter recommending the popular beverage. "If you are not feeling well, if you have not slept, chocolate will revive you. But you have no chocolate pot! I think of that again and again. How will you manage?"[8]

For people like the fashionable marquise, chocolate could not be served properly without tall, elegant cups made of china and gold and a special pot with a hole in the lid for the stirring stick. French aristocrats were as particular about the ceremony of drinking chocolate as were the Aztecs and Maya.

During the 1600s, chocolate was so popular in France, Spain, and Italy that it caused a minor controversy in the Roman Catholic Church. The issue involved the periods of fasting that devout Catholics observed before receiving

This engraving, based on a painting by Francois Boucher, shows chocolate being served at an elegant breakfast in France during the 1700s.

Communion. Liquids did not break the fast, but should thick and frothy chocolate be considered a liquid? This was a very important question because aristocrats often had a cup of chocolate before going to morning Mass. In fact, fashionable women in Spain and Mexico actually drank chocolate during the service. Although church authorities disagreed violently over the issue, it was finally decided that chocolate did not break the Communion fast.

When the chocolate fad reached England in the late 1600s, it took a new turn. Chocolate was consumed not only in fashionable private homes but also in public places. Shops devoted exclusively to serving chocolate began appearing in London. Londoners were already patronizing establishments that served another new beverage, coffee. This drink, introduced from the Arab world, was attracting great attention in Europe during the late 1600s, as was tea, a product of Asia. Europeans who had survived on beer, ale, and wine since medieval times now had three exotic new beverages to choose from.

The chocolate shops in England, like the coffee shops, catered to wealthy young men

In a book about coffee, tea, and chocolate published in 1688, Philippe Dufour pictured an Arab, a Chinese, and an Aztec, representing the three cultures that gave these exotic beverages to the world. A chocolate pot and the stirring stick known as a *molinet* are shown on the lower right.

who gathered there for amusement and good conversation. They read the paper, played cards, and talked about politics with their friends, all the while sipping cup after cup of expensive chocolate. The shops were something like private social clubs, with the same people meeting there night after night. Some of the patrons were literary men like Richard Steele, who in the early 1700s wrote articles for his fashionable newspaper the *Tatler* while seated at a table in White's Chocolate House.

Other activities taking place at the chocolate shops were less respectable. Young men gambled away their money there and got into fights over card games. White's Chocolate House became particularly known as a rowdy gaming spot. In 1733, the artist William Hogarth made a series of engravings called *The Rake's Progress*, which pictured a young man's scandalous life in London. He used White's as a background for one of the riotous gambling scenes.

By the end of the 1700s, chocolate was becoming more common in many European countries. Spain's monopoly on cacao seeds was long over. Now countries such as France, England, and Holland grew cacao in their colonies located in the East and West Indies, Africa, and other tropical regions. For the first time in its history, chocolate was coming within the reach of ordinary people.

The drink itself had gone through some changes since its arrival in Europe in the early 1500s. Water was no longer the only liquid with which it was made. Europeans dissolved cacao tablets in beer, ale, even wine, but milk was becoming more and more popular. Chocolate made with warm milk seemed particularly suited to children. Without all the spices and other ingredients used in earlier times, it was considered a soothing and nourishing drink for the young.

Up until the early 1800s, chocolate in Europe was basically what it had been in the Maya and Aztec worlds: a drink made from roasted and ground cacao seeds. The chocolate goodies that we know so well today—candy bars, fudge, brownies, chocolate-chip cookies—were unheard of. Although cacao paste was sometimes used as a cooking ingredient in the late 1700s, this was not very common. Most people simply did not think of chocolate as something to eat. But in 1828, the world of chocolate was changed forever. In that year, a Dutch chemist named Coenraad van Houten invented a new machine for processing cacao.

In their natural state, the seeds of the cacao tree contain a large amount of vegetable fat—at least 53 percent. For this reason, the chocolate drink that Aztecs and Europeans made from the ground seeds was very oily and rich. This fat content made chocolate nourishing, but it also made it fattening and sometimes hard to digest. Coenraad van Houten found a way to get rid of most of the fat in cacao seeds. He invented a screw press that crushed the ground seeds, squeezing out at least two-thirds of the fat. What was left, after a little additional processing, was cocoa powder, an entirely new product. (The word *cocoa* is a mixed-up version of *cacao*—another example of the confused, and confusing, names of things related to chocolate.)

The process that van Houten invented transformed cacao seeds into a product that was convenient and easy to use. But a byproduct of the process was all the fat that had been pressed out of the seeds. This yellowish, chocolaty-smelling fat, which today is known as cocoa butter, could not be wasted. So van Houten came up with the idea of *adding* the cocoa butter to another batch of ground cacao seeds, along with sugar and vanilla. When these ingredients were stirred together, they formed a mixture that was sweet and chocolaty. Further mixing, beating, and kneading made a smoother and

A box of Cadbury's cocoa from the late 1800s.

more delectable product. Van Houten had created the first eating chocolate—in other words, chocolate candy.

After Coenraad van Houten developed the basic process, many other people got on the chocolate bandwagon. Companies in Holland, England, and Switzerland began producing all kinds of eating chocolate, usually sold in the form of bars or slabs. Of course, they also made cocoa powder. European chocolate manufacturers such as Lindt, Fry, Tobler, and Nestlé all got their start in business during the 1800s. In 1875, a Swiss chocolate maker invented milk chocolate simply by adding condensed milk to the mixture of ground cacao, cocoa butter, and sugar.

A symbol of Baker's chocolate products since the late 1800s, this picture is based on a well-known painting from 1743 called *La Belle Chocolatière (The Beautiful Chocolate Girl).*

During the 1800s, chocolate manufacturing also became a thriving business in North America. People in the United States had always enjoyed drinking chocolate, just like their relatives in Europe. In fact, Thomas Jefferson had predicted in the late 1700s that "the superiority of chocolate, both for health and nourishment, will soon give it the same preference over tea and coffee in America which it has in Spain."[9]

In 1765, Dr. James Baker started a business grinding cacao seeds in a Massachusetts town. By the 1820s, the doctor's grandson, Walter Baker, was manufacturing the new chocolate products that had been made possible by van Houten's invention. Today the Baker Company is most famous for "baking" chocolate, named not in honor of the company founder but because it is used in making brownies, cakes, and other baked goods. (Baking chocolate is the purest form of chocolate available today; it is unsweetened cacao paste, with nothing added and nothing taken away.)

The biggest name in American chocolate, Hershey, did not get a start until the late 1800s. In 1893, Milton Hershey, a successful manufacturer of caramel candy in Lancaster, Pennsylvania, discovered the new world of chocolate at the Columbian Exposition held in Chicago. Here he saw equipment from Europe designed to process cacao seeds into smooth, sweet chocolate for eating. Hershey bought the equipment, took it home, and added chocolate-

In Hershey, Pennsylvania, the streetlamps are shaped like Kisses, the popular chocolate candies made by the Hershey Company.

making to his candy business. In 1900, he declared that "caramels are only a fad. Chocolate is a permanent thing."[10] From that time on, making chocolate was his only business.

Hershey's milk chocolate bars, made with fresh milk, were immediately popular, as was his cocoa powder. In 1907, the foil-wrapped little candies called Kisses began rolling off the production line of Hershey's Pennsylvania factory. This giant plant used the methods of mass production to turn out inexpensive chocolate products in large quantities. Next to his factory, Hershey built a company town, with houses for employees, schools, churches, even a zoo. Streets in Hershey were named Cocoa and Chocolate, and the streetlights were shaped like Kisses. Milton Hershey had created a self-contained world devoted to the manufacture of chocolate, a world that still exists today.

After chocolate was transformed by Coenraad van Houten in the early 1800s, it began a new career not only as candy but also as an ingredient in cooking. Cooks could now use chocolate in several different forms. Cocoa powder could be mixed with flour, sugar, butter, and eggs to make delicious tortes and cakes. Unsweetened baking chocolate, melted and combined with sugar, produced baked goods and other treats with an intense chocolate flavor. If cooks wanted chocolate that was already sweetened, they could choose from bars labeled bittersweet, semisweet, or sweet, depending on the amount of sugar they contained.

Just as the French had raised the drinking of chocolate to an art in the 1700s, they later became specialists in creating chocolate desserts. French cooks made chocolate mousse and chocolate soufflé, combining fluffy beaten eggs with the dense taste of chocolate. Pastry chefs turned out elegant multilayered chocolate cakes. Christmas was celebrated with *bûche de Noël*, a sponge cake made in the shape of a Yule log and covered with a "bark" of rich chocolate frosting. But chocolate treats were not just for special occasions. *Pain au chocolate*, a warm pastry with a piece of chocolate hidden inside it, became a favorite afternoon snack of French schoolchildren, and it still is.

During the 1800s, other European countries also created fabulous chocolate desserts. In Austria, pastry shops served slices of rich chocolate cakes and tortes topped with mounds of whipped cream. Austria's capital, Vienna, became the home of one of the world's most famous chocolate desserts, the Sacher torte. This dense chocolate cake glazed with apricot jam was first created in 1832 by a chef named Franz Sacher, who worked for an Austrian prince. Sacher later opened an elegant hotel in Vienna, where the popular torte was served. Today the Hotel Sacher still makes the Sacher torte and ships it to customers all over the world.

The United States had its own special treats featuring chocolate. The brownie is an American creation, as is the rich chocolate candy known as fudge. Another well-known American chocolate treat is the chocolate-chip cookie, which originated in 1930 at an old Massachusetts inn called the Toll House. Ruth Wakefield, the inn owner, made her cookies with chopped bar chocolate, but Toll House cookies became so popular that, in 1939, the Nestlé company created chocolate chips specifically for this use.

Today cooks in the United States have discovered so-called white chocolate as a cooking ingredient. White chocolate has only a mild chocolate taste, which is not surprising since its main ingredient is cocoa butter, the fat pressed from the cacao seeds in chocolate processing. For true "chocoholics," white chocolate is a pale reflection of the real thing.

In Mexico, where the story of chocolate began, rich chocolaty sweets are not common. Instead, chocolate is used in some unusual ways—for example, as part of the spicy *mole* sauces that are served with meats. Mexicans also drink a lot of chocolate, just as their Indian and Spanish ancestors did. They make it with prepared tablets containing cacao paste, sugar, cinnamon, and ground almonds. These tablets are dissolved in hot water or milk, and then the liquid is whipped vigorously with a special wooden beater, known in Mexico as a *molinillo*. Rich, sweet, and frothy, this chocolate drink combines traditions from two worlds.

OTHER FOODS FROM THE AMERICAS

Maize, potatoes, tomatoes, peanuts, chocolate, capsicum peppers, and the many varieties of American beans had a tremendous influence on cooking and eating around the world. Other food plants native to the Americas were not quite so influential. Some did not travel far beyond their original homes, while others became important only in certain regions. Yet even these less significant American foods had an impact on the everyday eating habits of people in many parts of the world.

Manioc.

For millions of people in Africa and South America today, manioc (also called cassava) is a staple food, yet most North Americans and Europeans have never even heard of it. The manioc plant originated in the tropical lowlands of South America, where ancient Native Americans used its thick, starch-filled roots as a source of food. Because some varieties of manioc contain prussic acid, a deadly poison, their roots have to be processed in a special way before they can be consumed. Native people grated the roots and then squeezed or pounded them to extract the poison. After drying, manioc became a kind of meal or flour that was used to make filling breads and porridges.

In 1492, Columbus found manioc growing in the Caribbean islands, and when he returned to Spain he took a supply of manioc bread with him to feed his crew. Later Europeans encountered manioc in South America during the early 1500s and were astonished by the ease with which the plant could be grown. Cuttings from a manioc stem could be put into the ground, and less than a year later, the plant roots would have grown to the size of a person's leg. Europeans were also impressed by the fact that manioc meal could be kept for several years without spoiling, although they did not care much for its bland taste.

The Portuguese brought manioc to Africa in the mid-1500s, and it was quickly accepted in tropical regions where other food plants were scarce. Africans were soon harvesting the roots and processing them in ways very similar to those used in South America. Today manioc products are an important part of the diet in many African countries. All over West Africa, people eat stews and soups along with *fufu*, dumplings made from cooked and mashed manioc. In Nigeria, toasted manioc meal, called *gari*, is a popular cooking ingredient.

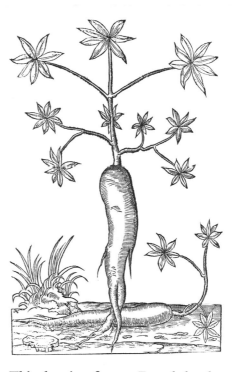

This drawing from a French book published in 1557 shows the thick roots of the manioc plant.

South Americans also eat manioc in many forms, including *farofa*, a toasted meal that is common in Brazilian cuisine. Even North Americans and Europeans sometimes consume manioc without knowing it. Tapioca, which is used to thicken puddings and sauces, is made from dried manioc.

Squash. In the 1500s, dozens of kinds of squashes were growing in the gardens of the Incas, Aztecs, Maya, and many of the native peoples of North America. Europeans recognized these American plants as relatives of familiar Old World natives such as cucumbers, melons (including cantaloupe and watermelon), and gourds, all members of the large scientific family Cucurbitaceae.

The American cucurbits, called *askutasquash* in an Algonquian language, included a bewildering number of varieties that were put to many different uses. Some of the plants produced hard-shelled fruits with succulent flesh that could be cooked in the shell or dried and preserved for future use. The dried shells themselves could be used as containers and ladles. Other New World cucurbits had soft, edible shells and were usually eaten fresh from the garden. The seeds and even the flowers of many of the plants were also used as food.

The pumpkin got its name from *pompion*, a French word for a kind of melon.

The pumpkin was the largest of the New World cucurbits. Native Americans cooked pumpkins whole in the ashes of a fire, scooped out the soft flesh, and ate it sweetened with maple syrup. European settlers in North America at first used this same cooking method and later combined pumpkin with milk, eggs, and molasses to make a filling for a European-style pie.

Today the pumpkin and most of its close relatives in the squash tribe (acorn, Hubbard, butternut, crookneck, etc.) are not very well known outside of the Americas. The one exception is the zucchini, an American squash that goes by an Italian name. This soft-shelled variety was taken to Italy during the 1600s and became very popular there. Later reintroduced to North America, the prolific but rather tasteless zucchini has now taken over many backyard gardens and turns up in all kinds of dishes, from casseroles to omelets to cookies.

Pineapple. Of all the food plants of the Americas, the pineapple was the one that at first seemed to impress Europeans most. They described the taste of the juicy New World fruit as a delectable blend of melons and peaches. Native to the hot humid regions of South America, pineapples spread to Mexico and the West Indies, where they were cultivated in ancient times. During his second expedition to the Caribbean in 1493, Columbus sampled the exotic fruit, called *annani* by the native people. Spaniards called the fruit *piñas* because of its resemblance to a pinecone. The English name had the same origin, although the French word *anana* preserved the original native name.

When pineapples were first shipped to Europe in the 1500s, few survived the long voyage. Those that did arrive unspoiled were presented to monarchs and nobles, and the European pineapple craze began. Pineapples became a luxury food item for the well-to-do, particularly in England. During the 1700s, members of the English nobility grew the tropical fruit in special greenhouses called pineries. An ambitious hostess could even rent a pineapple

In a book about the West Indies published in 1535, Gonzalo Fernandez de Oviedo introduced Europeans to the sweet, juicy pineapple.

to use as a centerpiece for an elegant dinner table. The American fruit was so cherished that it became a symbol of wealth and hospitality, its image carved in wood on doorways and bedposts.

By the 1800s, the pineapple was not such a rare and expensive commodity. The fruit was much more widely available, grown not only in the Americas but also in Australia, Asia, and Africa. In the 1880s, the first large pineapple plantations were established in the Hawaiian Islands. Today, the

Asian country of Thailand is the largest producer of pineapples, growing about one-quarter of the world supply. No longer a food of the privileged and wealthy, pineapple in cans can be found on grocery shelves just about anywhere.

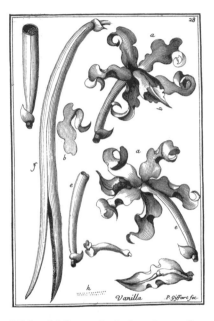

This old botanical drawing of the vanilla orchid pictures the delicate flower (a) and the long seed pod (f), which must be fermented to produce the familiar vanilla flavor.

Vanilla. When Aztec cooks made the cacao drink *cacaoatl*, one of the flavorings they often added was *tlilxochitl*, made from the seedpod of an orchid plant. This exotic-sounding ingredient is today's vanilla, one of the most common flavorings in the modern world. The Aztecs obtained *tlilxochitl* from the Totonac people, who lived on Mexico's Gulf coast. It was the Totonacs who had discovered how to cultivate one special orchid plant and to process its long, slender seedpods to produce the fragrant seasoning. When the Aztecs conquered the Totonacs in the 1400s, they demanded *tlilxochitl* as tribute from their subjects.

Spainards called the delicious seasoning *vainilla*, a word meaning "little pod." They imported it to Europe, along with cacao, and for many years, vanilla (the English spelling of the word) was used only to flavor chocolate beverages. Gradually, however, Europeans and Asians discovered that it could add a subtle flavor to many different dishes.

Cultivation of vanilla outside of Mexico became possible in the 1800s when a Belgian botanist learned how to pollinate the orchid flowers by hand. Before that time, vanilla orchids grown in other areas did not reproduce well because the bees and hummingbirds that pollinated the flowers in

Mexico were not present. After the development of hand-pollination, the French, who were very fond of vanilla, established plantations of vanilla orchids in their colonies in tropical regions.

Vanilla became more convenient to use in 1847, when an American discovered how to extract the vanilla flavor by soaking chopped-up pods in a mixture of alcohol and water. Today vanilla extract is commonly used in the United States, although many Europeans cooks still prefer the whole pod. Also common today is synthetic vanilla, made by a chemical process. This artificial product, however, can't match the sweet, delicate flavor of natural vanilla first discovered by the people of ancient America.

Avocado. Another food plant that Native Americans gave to the world is the avocado, which was grown by the Aztecs. The English name for the plant comes from the Nahuatl word *ahuacatl*, and the most common modern way of serving avocados—mashed and seasoned as guacamole—is also Aztec in name and origin. Aztec cooks made an avocado sauce called *ahuaca-mulli*, which was no doubt eaten with maize tortillas, just as people today scoop up guacamole with tortilla chips.

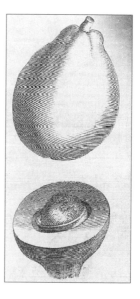

When Spaniards in Mexico tasted the avocado, they were intrigued by its buttery flavor and by the large amount of oil it contained. (Only the olive and the coconut contain as much vegetable oil as the avocado.) Some Spaniards ate the exotic New World fruit seasoned with salt, while others thought that, with the addition of a little sugar, it made a fine dessert.

The rich, oily avocado reminded some Europeans of the olives that were so important in the cooking of southern Europe.

The avocado was too fragile to survive the trip to Europe well, and it remained mainly an American food until the 1900s, when better methods of shipment and storage were developed. Today it is known in Europe, Africa, and Asia, often under the name alligator pear in honor of its rough skin and pearlike shape. Most of the world's avocados are still grown in the Americas, with the United States, Mexico, and Brazil the top producers.

American Nuts.

The peanut, the most important American "nut," is actually a legume, but at least one true nut from the Americas has traveled abroad. That is the cashew, a native of tropical South America now grown in Asia and Africa. Cashew nuts come from trees in the same scientific family as the mango and the pistachio, as well as poison oak and poison ivy. The kidney-shaped nuts grow at the base of the juicy yellow or red cashew "apple," which is not a fruit at all but the enlarged stalk of the plant's flower. The nut itself, with its smooth shell enclosing a white kernel, is the actual fruit of the cashew tree.

As this drawing from the 1600s illustrates, the cashew nut grows at the base of a fleshy "apple."

In ancient times, the native people of Brazil grew cashew trees, which they called *acajú*, and used both the apples and the nuts as food. When the Portuguese discovered this unusual food plant, they shortened its name to *cajú* and carried the nuts with them to East Africa, India, and other parts of Asia. Cashew trees became established in these areas, and today India is the world's leading producer of cashews, followed by the African countries of Mozambique and Tanzania.

Unlike the American peanut, the cashew never became an important ingredient in the world diet. Today it is eaten mainly as a salted nut or used in candies. In most parts of the world, the cashew apple is discarded, although in Brazil, people drink cashew-apple juice, while in parts of India and Africa, the juice is used to make alcoholic beverages. Another unusual product of the cashew tree is CNSL (Cashew Nut Shell Liquid), an oily liquid derived from the nut shell lining. Extremely irritating to human skin (like the sap of poison oak and ivy), this liquid is removed from the shells by roasting and used for various industrial purposes. CNSL is an ingredient in some paints and varnishes, as well as in resins used in the brake linings of cars.

In addition to the cashew, a few other true nuts such as the pecan, the hickory, the Brazil nut, and the black walnut are native to the Americas. Most of these, however, did not leave home and even today are little known in other parts of the world.

American Berries. Berries gathered from wild plants were important in the diet of many native people in the Americas. In North America, cranberries, blueberries, strawberries, and many other varieties were eaten fresh or preserved by drying. Cranberries, called *ibimi* ("bitter berry") by the Algonquin people, were often cooked with venison meat and fat to make *pemmican*, a nourishing dried food that kept for months without spoiling.

European settlers in the Americas recognized many of the New World berries as close relatives of familiar varieties back home. (For example, the lingonberry, native to the Scandinavian countries, is a kind of cranberry.) But the American berries were often bigger and more productive than their Old World cousins. This was particularly true of the strawberry, which grew wild in many parts of the Americas and had been domesticated by native people in South America.

The strawberries that had been grown in Europe for centuries were developed from a wild wood strawberry that had a sweet flavor but was very small. During the 1600s and 1700s, several larger American strawberry varieties were imported to Europe, but they did not do well in their new homes. In the mid-1700s, after much experimentation, European botanists finally

developed a large, tasty hybrid strawberry by crossing two different American varieties, one from North America and one from South America. This new American berry is the ancestor of most cultivated strawberries grown around the world today.

This small, sweet strawberry was common in Europe during the 1500s. Most of today's strawberries were developed from larger varieties native to the Americas.

NOTES

INTRODUCTION

1. *The Log of Christopher Columbus*, translated by Robert H. Fuson (Camden, Maine: International Marine Publishing, 1992), 85.
2. Bernardino de Sahagún, *General History of the Things of New Spain*, translated by Arthur J. O. Anderson and Charles E. Dibble, in thirteen parts (Santa Fe, N.Mex.: School of American Research and the University of Utah, 1950–1982), 13:81.

MAIZE—THE AMERICAN GRAIN

1. Quoted in Betty Fussell, *The Story of Corn* (New York: Alfred A. Knopf, 1992), 17.
2. *The Life of the Admiral Christopher Columbus by his Son Ferdinand*, translated and annotated by Benjamin Keen (New Brunswick, N.J.: Rutgers University Press, 1959), 70.
3. Sahagún, 10:69.
4. Quoted in *Chilies to Chocolate: Food the Americas Gave the World*, edited by Nelson Foster and Linda S. Cardell (Tucson: University of Arizona Press, 1992), 54.
5. Sahagún, 10:42. Bernardino de Sahagún was a Franciscan friar, or brother, who came to Mexico from Spain in 1529. To aid in converting the conquered Aztec people to Roman Catholicism, Friar Sahagún set out to learn as much as he could about their language and culture. He interviewed many native people, asking detailed questions about Aztec history, religious beliefs, and social customs and writing down the answers in both Spanish and Nahuatl, the Aztec language. Sahagún also commissioned native artists to draw pictures representing different aspects of Aztec life. He combined all this material in a massive manuscript called *General History of the Things of New Spain*. (It is also known as the Florentine Codex because the most complete surviving copy is kept in a library in Florence, Italy.) Friar Sahagún's work provides invaluable information about Aztec civilization, including many fascinating details about agriculture, diet, and food preparation.
6. Gilbert L. Wilson, *Buffalo Bird Woman's Garden: Agriculture of the Hidatsa Indians* (St. Paul, Minn.: Minnesota Historical Society Press, 1987), 27.
7. Sahagún, 10:42.
8. Ibid., 69.
9. Bernabe Cobo, *History of the Inca Empire*, translated and edited by Roland Hamilton

(Austin: University of Texas Press, 1979), 28. *Chicha* was originally a Caribbean word for a beer made out of maize. Spaniards learned the word in the West Indies and used it to refer to other intoxicating maize beverages that they encountered in the New World. The Inca name for maize beer has been forgotten.

10. Pones and hoecakes were breads made out of maize ground into a meal or flour but without the addition of yeast or other leavening agents. The name *pone* comes from *apone*, a word in an Algonquian Indian language. Hoecakes got their name because they were often cooked on the metal blade of a hoe propped up at the edge of a fire. Johnnycake is another name that European settlers in North America used for this very basic Native American dish.

11. *Gerard's Herball: The Essence thereof distilled* by Marcus Woodward (London: Gerald Howe, Publisher, 1927), 26. During the 1500s and 1600s, many illustrated books called herbals were published in Europe. They combined botanical information about plants with descriptions of their use in medical treatment. Today herbals provide the earliest written accounts of the arrival of American plants in Europe. Some herbal writers were scientists who possessed great knowledge of plants, while others were enthusiastic amateurs. The English writer John Gerard belongs to the second group, but his book gives us valuable information about the way that Europeans saw these strange plants from a new world.

12. Quoted in Alfred Crosby, Jr., *The Columbian Exchange: Biological and Cultural Consequences of 1492* (Westport, Conn.: Greenwood Press, 1973), 179.

13. Quoted in Fussell, 235.

BEANS—NEW VARIETIES FROM A NEW WORLD

1. *The Log of Christopher Columbus*, 85.

2. Other more modern sayings about beans seem to put a higher value on them. For example, "full of beans," which probably originated in the United States during the 1870s, is used to describe a person who is brimming with energy and high spirits.

3. Sahagún, 11:284.

4. Ibid., 10:70.

5. Today beans are usually classified into three different groups, depending on the stage of development in which they are cooked and eaten. String beans, or snap beans, are eaten whole when the pods are still young and tender. When the pods become older and tougher, the still tender seeds inside are removed and eaten as shell beans. The dried seeds of fully developed beans make up the third and most common category of bean usage.

6. To reduce the problem of flatulence, experts suggest soaking beans before cooking them in fresh water. Eating beans more often also helps because the digestive system gets used to dealing with the complex sugars they contain.

PEPPERS—HOT AND SWEET

1. *The Log of Christopher Columbus*, 175.
2. Sahagún, 10:67.
3. *The Log of Christopher Columbus*, 175.
4. Michele de Cuneo's Letter on the Second Voyage, 28 October 1495, in *Journals and Other Documents on the Life and Voyage of Christopher Columbus*, translated and edited by Samuel Eliot Morison (New York: Heritage Press, 1963), 216.
5. Quoted in Jean Andrews, *Red Hot Peppers* (New York: Macmillan Publishing Company, 1993), 61.
6. Sahagún, 8:37.
7. Ibid., 10:70.
8. Quoted in Jean Andrews, *Peppers: The Domesticated Capsicums* (Austin: University of Texas Press, 1984), 25.

PEANUTS—FROM THE AMERICAS TO AFRICA AND BACK AGAIN

1. Sahagún, 10.85–86.
2. Quoted in Frederic Rosengarten, Jr., *The Book of Edible Nuts* (New York: Walker and Company, 1984), 146.
3. Sophie Coe, *America's First Cuisines* (Austin: University of Texas Press, 1994), 35.
4. For additional information about this trans-Pacific trade route, which linked Europe and Asia by way of the Americas, see Eugene Lyon's "Track of the Manila Galleons," *National Geographic* (September 1990), 5–37.
5. *Popular Songs of 19th Century America*, selected by Richard Jackson (New York: Dover Publications, 1976), 74-75.

POTATOES—BURIED TREASURE

1. Cobo, 185.
2. The Spaniards were very impressed when they saw the hundreds of terraced fields in Peru. Andes, the Spanish name for the lofty mountains, comes from *andanes*, a word meaning terraces or platforms.
3. Cobo, 28.
4. Ibid., 192.

5. Quoted in Redcliffe N. Salaman, *The History and Social Influence of the Potato* (Cambridge, England: Cambridge University Press, 1949), 102.

6. Ibid.

7. Quoted in E. J. Kahn, Jr., *The Staffs of Life* (Boston: Little, Brown and Company, 1985), 110. The truffle connection survived even after potatoes became better known in Europe. In several European languages, the earliest name for the potato was derived from words meaning "truffle." In Italy, the truffle was *tartufi*, and the potato was called *tartuffo*. Germans knew the American potato as *kartoffel*, while in the Russian language, it became *kartopfel*. Some of these names are still used today.

8. *Gerard's Herball*, 222–223.

9. Ibid., 223.

10. Quoted in Coe, 19.

11. Quoted in Salaman, 108.

12. Quoted in Crosby, 182. This unflattering description of the potato appeared in the encyclopedia compiled by the French philosopher and writer Denis Diderot in the mid-1700s.

13. Redcliffe N. Salaman devotes many pages of his monumental work to the "social influence" of the potato. Other books that cover this subject in less detail are *The Columbian Exchange* by Alfred Crosby and *Indian Givers: How the Indians of the Americas Transformed the World* by Jack Weatherford (New York: Ballantine Books, 1988).

14. Quoted in Kahn, 120.

15. Salaman, 300. Later research proved that the Irish potatoes had been attacked by a plant fungus whose scientific name is *Phytophthora infestans*. The destruction was so widespread because only a few varieties of potatoes were grown in Ireland, and none was resistant to the fungus. Since the time of the Potato Famine, potato varieties have been developed that are not so susceptible to this devastating plant disease, which is commonly known as "early blight." Modern chemical fungicides have also helped to control the disease.

TOMATOES—FORBIDDEN FRUIT

1. Sahagún, 10:70.

2. Ibid., 68.

3. In *America's First Cuisines*, Sophie Coe gives a good description of the different *-tomatls* grown by the Aztecs and the confusion that resulted when the Spaniards called them all *tomates* (46–47).

4. Andrew F. Smith, *The Tomato in America: Early History, Culture, and Cookery* (Columbia, S.C.: University of South Carolina Press, 1994), 12–13.

5. *Gerard's Herball*, 79, 81.

6. Rudolf Grewe, "The Arrival of the Tomato in Spain and Italy: Early Recipes," *Journal of Gastronomy* (summer 1987), 67–82.

7. Ibid., 69.

8. Raymond Sokolov describes how the tomato transformed gazpacho in his book *Why We Eat What We Eat* (New York: Summit Books, 1991), 116–120.

9. The facts behind the Johnson legend can be found in Smith, *The Tomato in America*, 3–8.

10. For more information on the history of the world's most famous tomato sauce, see Raymond Sokolov's article "Sauce for the Masses," *Natural History* (May 1984), 90–95.

CHOCOLATE—FOOD OF THE GODS

1. Girolamo Benzoni, *History of the New World* (New York: Burt Franklin, Publishers, 1857), 150.

2. Ibid.

3. You can find a brief note about the Maya pottery vessel that contained cacao in *National Geographic* (March 1991), Geographica section.

4. Diego Duran, *The Aztecs* (New York: Orion Press, 1964), 266. Historians and linguists disagree over the origin of the European word *chocolate* and even over the different Nahuatl words for "chocolate" products. Some think that the Aztecs did not call their cacao drink *cacaoatl* (cacao water) but *xocoatl* (bitter water) and that this is the origin of the Spanish/English word *chocolate*. A few people have even suggested that the word *chocolate* is derived from the sound ("choco, choco, choco") made by beating and stirring the cacao beverage.

5. Bernal Díaz del Castillo, *The Discovery and Conquest of Mexico,* translated by A. O. Maudslay (New York: Grove Press, 1956), 210–211.

6. Sahagún, 10:93.

7. Ibid.

8. Quoted in Maguelonne Touissant-Samat, *A History of Food*, translated from the French by Anthea Bell (Cambridge, Mass.: Blackwell Publishers, 1992), 574.

9. Quoted in Marcia and Frederic Morton, *Chocolate: An Illustrated History* (New York: Crown Publishers, 1986), 34.

10. Ibid., 73

BIBLIOGRAPHY

Note: The starred books (★) will be of particular interest to young readers.

★Ammon, Richard. *The Kids' Book of Chocolate*. New York: Atheneum, 1987.

Andrews, Jean. *Peppers: The Domesticated Capsicums*. Austin: University of Texas Press, 1984.

★————. *Red Hot Peppers*. New York: Macmillan Publishing Company, 1993.

Arber, Agnes. *Herbals: Their Origin and Evolution*. Darien, Conn.: Hafner Publishing Company, 1970.

Baggett, Nancy. *International Chocolate Cookbook*. New York: Stewart Tabori & Chang, 1991.

Benzoni, Girolamo. *History of the New World*. New York: Burt Franklin, Publishers, 1857.

★Berdan, Frances F. *The Aztecs*. New York: Chelsea House Publishers, 1989.

★Busenberg, Bonnie. *Vanilla, Chocolate, & Strawberry: The Story of Your Favorite Flavors*. Minneapolis: Lerner Publications Company, 1994.

Cobo, Bernabe. *History of the Inca Empire*. Translated and edited by Roland Hamilton. Austin: University of Texas Press, 1979.

★Coe, Sophie. *America's First Cuisines*. Austin: University of Texas Press, 1994.

Cosman, Madeline Pelner. *Fabulous Feasts: Medieval Cookery and Ceremony*. New York: George Braziller, 1976.

★Crosby, Alfred, Jr. *The Columbian Exchange: Biological and Cultural Consequences of 1492*. Westport, Conn.: Greenwood Press, 1973.

Díaz del Castillo, Bernal. *The Discovery and Conquest of Mexico*. Translated by A. O. Maudslay. New York: Grove Press, Inc., 1956.

Duran, Diego. *The Aztecs*. New York: Orion Press, 1964.

★Foster, Nelson, and Linda S. Cardell, eds. *Chilies to Chocolate: Food the Americas Gave the World*. Tucson: University of Arizona Press, 1992.

Fuson, Robert H., trans. *The Log of Christopher Columbus*. Camden, Maine: International Marine Publishing, 1992.

★Fussell, Betty. *The Story of Corn*. New York: Alfred A. Knopf, 1992.

Garland, Sarah. *The Complete Book of Herbs and Spices*. Pleasantville, N.Y.: Reader's Digest Association, 1993.

Grant, Rosamund. *Caribbean and African Cooking*. New York: Interlink Books, 1993.

Grewe, Rudolf. "The Arrival of the Tomato in Spain and Italy: Early Recipes," *Journal of Gastronomy* (summer 1987): 67–82.

*Hafner, Dorinda. *A Taste of Africa*. Berkeley, Calif.: Ten Speed Press, 1993.

*Harris, Jessica B. *Iron Pots and Wooden Spoons: Africa's Gift to New World Cooking*. New York: Atheneum, 1989.

*———. *The Welcome Table: African-American Heritage Cooking*. New York: Simon & Schuster, 1995.

Heiser, Charles B., Jr. *Seed to Civilization: The Story of Food*. Cambridge, Mass.: Harvard University Press, 1990.

Herbert, John P. *1492: An Ongoing Voyage*. Washington, D.C.: Library of Congress, 1992.

Hobhouse, Henry. *Seeds of Change: Five Plants That Transformed Mankind*. New York: Harper & Row, 1986.

Hultman, Tami, ed. *Africa News Cookbook*. New York: Viking Penguin, 1985.

Jackson, Richard, ed. *Popular Songs of 19th Century America*. New York: Dover Publications, 1976.

Jaffrey, Madhur. *Madhur Jaffrey's Far Eastern Cookery*. New York: Harper & Row, 1989.

Kahn, E. J., Jr. *The Staffs of Life*. Boston: Little, Brown and Company, 1985.

Kaplan, Lawrence. "New World Beans," *Horticulture* (October 1980): 44–49.

Keen, Benjamin, trans. *The Life of the Admiral Christopher Columbus by his Son Ferdinand*. New Brunswick, N.J.: Rutgers University Press, 1959.

Kennedy, Diana. *The Cuisines of Mexico*. New York: Harper & Row, 1986.

Law, Ruth. *Southeast Asia Cookbook*. New York: Donald I. Fine, 1990.

*London, Sheryl, and Mel London. *The Versatile Grain and the Elegant Bean: A Celebration of the World's Most Healthful Foods*. New York: Simon & Schuster, 1992.

Luard, Elisabeth. *The Old World Kitchen: The Rich Tradition of European Peasant Cooking*. New York: Bantam Books, 1987.

Lyon, Eugene. "Track of the Manila Galleons," *National Geographic* (September 1990), 5–37.

*Marrin, Albert. *Aztecs and Spaniards: Cortés and the Conquest of Mexico*. New York: Atheneum, 1986.

*———. *Inca and Spaniard: Pizarro and the Conquest of Peru*. New York: Atheneum, 1989.

Medearis, Angela. *African-American Kitchen*. New York: Dutton/Penguin Group, 1994.

*Meyer, Carolyn, and Charles Gallenkamp, *The Mystery of the Ancient Maya*. New York: Margaret K. McElderry Books, 1995.

Milanich, Jerald T., and Susan Milbrath, eds. *First Encounters: Spanish Exploration in the Caribbean and the United States, 1492–1570*. Gainesville: University of Florida Press, 1989.

*Miller, Mark. *Great Chile Book*. Berkeley, Calif.: Ten Speed Press, 1991.

Morison, Samuel Eliot, trans. and ed. "Michele de Cuneo's Letter on the Second Voyage, 28 October 1495." *Journals and Other Documents on the Life and Voyage of Christopher Columbus*. New York: Heritage Press, 1963.

BIBLIOGRAPHY

★Morton, Marcia, and Frederic Morton. *Chocolate: An Illustrated History*. New York: Crown Publishers, 1986.

Mosley, Michael E. *The Inca and Their Ancestors: The Archaeology of Peru*. London: Thames & Hudson, 1992.

Phillips, William D., Jr., and Carla Rahn Phillips. *The Worlds of Christopher Columbus*. Cambridge, England: Cambridge University Press, 1992.

★Rahn, Joan Elma. *Plants That Changed History*. New York: Atheneum, 1982.

Reveal, James L. *Gentle Conquest: The Botanical Discovery of North America with Illustrations from the Library of Congress*. Washington, D.C.: Starwood Publishing, 1992.

Rosengarten, Frederic, Jr. *The Book of Edible Nuts*. New York: Walker and Company, 1984.

★Rosin, Elizabeth. *Blue Corn and Chocolate*. New York: Alfred A. Knopf, 1992.

★Rupp, Rebecca. *Blue Corn and Square Tomatoes*. Pownal, Vt.: Storey Communications, 1987.

Sahagún, Bernardino de. *General History of the Things of New Spain*. Translated by Arthur J. O. Anderson and Charles E. Dibble, in thirteen parts. Santa Fe, N.Mex.: School of American Research and the University of Utah, 1950-1982.

Salaman, Redcliffe N. *The History and Social Influence of the Potato*. Cambridge, England: Cambridge University Press, 1949.

Smith, Andrew F. *The Tomato in America: Early History, Culture, and Cookery*. Columbia, S.C.: University of South Carolina Press, 1994.

Sokolov, Raymond. "Sauce for the Masses," *Natural History* (May 1984): 90–95.

★Sokolov, Raymond. *Why We Eat What We Eat*. New York: Summit Books, 1991.

Tannahill, Reay. *Food in History*. New York: Crown Publishers, 1988.

Touissant-Samat, Maguelonne. *A History of Food*. Translated from the French by Anthea Bell. Cambridge, Mass.: Blackwell Publishers, 1992.

Tyler, S. Lyman. *The Indian Encounter with the European, 1492–1509*. Salt Lake City: University of Utah Press, 1988.

★Viola, Herman J., and Carolyn Margolis, eds. *Seeds of Change*. Washington, D.C.: Smithsonian Institution Press, 1991.

★Weatherford, Jack. *Indian Givers: How the Indians of the Americas Transformed the World*. New York: Ballantine Books, 1988.

★———. *Native Roots: How the Indians Enriched America*. New York: Ballantine Books, 1991.

★Wells, Troth. *The World in Your Kitchen*. Freedom, Calif.: Crossing Press, 1993.

Wilson, Gilbert L. *Buffalo Bird Woman's Garden: Agriculture of the Hidatsa Indians*. St. Paul, Minn.: Minnesota Historical Society Press, 1987.

Woodward, Marcus. *Gerard's Herball: The Essence thereof distilled*. London: Gerald Howe, Publisher, 1927.

ABOUT THE ILLUSTRATIONS

Many of the illustrations in this book are reprinted from books published in Europe during the 1500s and 1600s, at the very time the Old World and the New World were discovering each other. Some are accounts of European exploration and settlement in the Americas. Others are books about plants that include exotic American species such as maize and potatoes. I was lucky enough to find copies of these precious old books in libraries at the University of Minnesota, where I spent many hours carefully turning the time-worn pages and gazing in awe at the wonderful illustrations. Following is a list of the pictures that I selected to use and the books from which they were obtained (be sure to notice the dates of publication). Also listed are other illustration sources.

Illustrations reprinted from books in the collections of the following libraries at the University of Minnesota:

James Ford Bell Library: pp. ii–iii, 68, from Caspar Plautius, *Nova typis trans acta navigation*, 1621; pp. 1, 103, from Philippe Dufour, *Traitez nouveaux & curieux du café, du thé, et du chocolate*, 1688; pp. 3, 8, 12, 13, from Theodor de Bry, *Reisen im Occidentalischen Indien*, 1590; p. 7, from Giovanni Battista Ramusio, *Delle navigationi et viaggi*, 1606; p. 15, from Girolamo Benzoni, *La historia del mondo nuovo*, 1565; p. 22, from Francis Moore, *Travels in Inland Parts of Africa*, 1738; p. 41, from Abraham Ortelius, *Theatrum orbis terrarum*, 1570; p. 59, from Willem Bosman, *Naukeurige beschrying van de Goud-Tand-en Slave-Kust*, 1709; pp. 96, 116, from Charles de Rocheforte, *Histoire naturelle et morale des iles Antilles de l'Amerique*, 1681; p. 111, from Andre Thevet, *Les singularitez de la France antarctique*, 1557; p. 113, from Gonzalo Fernandez de Oviedo y Valdes, *La historia general de la Indias*, 1535; p. 115, from Jean Baptiste Labat, *Nouveau voyage aux isles de l'Amerique*, 1722.

Wangensteen Historical Library of Biology and Medicine, Biomedical Library: pp. vi, 19, 27, 46, 69, 88, from John Gerard, *The Herbal, or General Historie of Plantes. Very much enlarged and amended by Thomas Johnson*, 1636; pp. 17, 32, 45, from Leonhart Fuchs, *Den nieuwen herbarius*, 1543; pp. 33, 40, 70, 74, from Carolus Clusius (Charles L'Ecluse), *Rariorum plantarum historica*, 1601; pp. 53, 100, from Willem Piso, *De Indiae Utriusque re Naturali et Medica*, 1658; pp. 73, 86, from Basil Besler, *Hortus eystettensis*, 1613; p. 114, from Charles Plumier, *Nova Plantarum Americanarum*, 1703; p. 118, from Hieronymus Bock, *Kreuter buch*, 1551.

Anderson Horticulture Library: pp. 47, 112, from James Vicks, *Seedsman Catalog*, Rochester, N.Y., 1891; p. 92, from John Lewis Childs, *Spring Catalogue of Seeds, Bulbs and Plants for 1889.*

Wilson Library: p. 61 *Scientific American*, December 29, 1894; p. 80, *Illustrated London News*, December 22, 1849; p. 81, *Illustrated London News*, May 10, 1851.

Other illustrations courtesy of: pp. 5, 6, 10, 30, 39, 98, from Bernardino de Sahagún, *General History of the Things of New Spain*, University of Utah Press, 1950-1982; pp. 9, 66, 67, from Felipe Guaman Poma de Ayala, *Nueva Coronica Y Buen Gobierno*, Institut d'Ethnologie, 1936; pp. 23, 25, 35, 48, 57, 82, 94, Food and Agriculture Organization of the United Nations; p. 29, Buckingham Collection, 1955.2274. Photograph by Christopher Gallagher, © 1995, The Art Institute of Chicago; pp. 34, 37, Northrup King Company Records, Minnesota Historical Society; p. 50 (top), McIlhenny Company; p. 50 (bottom), McCormick & Company, Inc.; p. 52, Dept. of Library Services, American Museum of Natural History (neg. #333990); p. 54, Peanut Advisory Board; p. 62, Tuskegee University; p. 65, University of Pennsylvania Museum, Philadelphia (neg. #39-20-32); p. 77, Bettmann Archives; p. 93, H.J. Heinz Company; p. 102, Metropolitan Museum of Art, the Elisha Whittelsey Fund, 1950 (50.567.34); p. 105, Cadbury Ltd.; p. 106, Kraft Foods, Inc. (registered trademark); p. 107,Richard Ammon and Darrell Peterson.

INDEX

INDEX